A tale of love, struggles and survival amidst war, social, and economic turmoil. Three countries, three generations and three families whose fates were intertwined by history and circumstances.

GERMAN P. PALABYAB

Author

Published by German P. Palabyab

Distributed by Kindle e-Books

The Saga of Leyte Gulf…

To my wife Lina Tantuico-Palabyab and my Filipino-American Children Mariquit, Ligaya, Isagani, Dalisay, Amihan, Josemaria, Mutya and Alvaro.

And

to All Filipino-Americans

FOREWORD

This is a story of love and betrayal; struggles and overcoming; and victories and defeat among three generations, three families and three countries.

Leyte Gulf had many historical stories and folktales that continue to impact our lives. This historical fiction dramatizes the stories of three generations of Filipino-Americans that were deeply intertwined with the historical events in Leyte Gulf and America. The Battle of Leyte Gulf, the greatest naval battle ever and the Leyte Landings in 1944 were the disruptive events that shaped the plot of this fiction. This is a fictional story of the social, cultural, economic and political issues the First Wave, up to the Post Millennial generations of Filipino-Americans struggled with in their adopted land. The fiction brings the reader back to the Post Depression, War Time, Pre-Civil Rights Movement and Post-War periods in America and the Philippines. It also highlighted how the "special relations" between the Philippines and the United

States of America developed. It attempts to bridge the information gap between the Post-Millennial Filipino-Americans and the older Filipino-American generations. It also hopes to connect them with their roots. Most of all, the fiction should be informative and yet enjoyable to read for any reader who is interested in World War II stories.

This author was driven to write this historical fiction to inform and educate the reader the importance of the historical events that happened in Leyte and Samar. This is especially true for immigrants and Filipino-American families because this is their story. We took great pains in seeing to it that our historical facts are accurate. This writer used real historical figures and personalities to interact with our main fictional characters. All references to Gen. Douglas MacArthur, the Leyte Landings and the Battle of Leyte Gulf are therefore factual and authentic. The physical and time setting of the story were actual places and events that really happened.

This is a story about love, betrayal, heroism and redemption involving three families, three generations and from three countries (Philippines, USA and Japan).

It is said that the best way to tell a real-life story of people and events is to dramatize and romanticize it.

This writer made an effort to put life to and dramatize the great events in Leyte like the Leyte landings, the Battle at Breakneck Ridge and of course the Battle of Leyte Gulf by romanticizing it with fictional characters who fell in love, who were betrayed and who did heroic acts that would otherwise just be lost in a plain documentary narrative.

The author also attempted to deliver his message about the social, political and economic issues that the immigrants struggled with in America during the Great Depression, racial discrimination, Pre-Civil Rights Movement, the war in the Pacific, and the post-war rehabilitation periods by dramatizing it through the story's fictional characters. The characters are fiction but the events, circumstances and setting are very authentic. Our honest and frank portrayal of the "special relations" between the Philippines and America were not meant to inflame feelings. The author merely wants to present a more objective account of how this Philippines-USA special relations came to be. For sure it is not what we were told by our elders. Be that as it may, we still value the relationship and we are grateful to America for their great contribution to Philippine history and culture. But we have to outgrow our old and traditional perception of America and begin to realize that we are now a sovereign country and our politics and interests are our own and separate. We have to out-grow being the little brother of big-brother America. – GPP

ACKNOWLEDGEMENT

It would have been monumentally difficult to write this book without the inspiration and help of some special people, their works and excellent reference materials. I am therefore grateful to the following people:

To my wife *Lina Hatton Tantuico Palabyab*, who's incessant prodding pushed me to write this book. Her maternal grandparents from the Hills and the Hattons descended from two American soldiers/volunteers who were members of an engineering battalion sent to Samar during the tenure of Gen. Arthur MacArthur as Governor-general. This was during the Filipino-American war that ended in 1902. They came down to Samar and Leyte to build roads and bridges.

To the late *Francisco S. Tantuico*, author, poet and public servant, who gave me a copy of his book "Leyte, Historic Islands" (1960) that gave me a lot of valuable historical facts about Leyte and from his excellent reference materials from his private library.

He gave me the impetus to write a book of my own;

To the late *Samuel Eliot Morison,* Trumbull Professor of American History of Harvard, Rear Admiral of the US Navy (Ret.) whose book "Leyte, June 1944-January 1945" (1963) was our source of reference for the detailed and official accounts of the Battle of Leyte Gulf;

To my colleagues and fellow government servants who served in Eastern Visayas and the people of Eastern Visayas Region who gave me first-hand accounts of some of the notable events that happened in Leyte and the very important folktales that were passed-on only by word of mouth;

To Wikipedia that afforded the author the facility and luxury of instantaneous fact checking;

Last but not least, to Aries Balanay and his Folium Multimedia Production team who helped me finalize the pre-press production of this book.

CONTENTS

INTRODUCTION

Come October 19 to 26, 2019 the Philippines and the United States of America, together with its allies at the Pacific theatre of the 2nd World War (Great Britain, Australia, Canada, Netherlands, New Zealand, and Taiwan) will celebrate the 75th Anniversary of the *Battle of Leyte Gulf and the Leyte Landings* respectively. Japan has always been a special guest to these historical events too because as time healed old wounds, friendship and goodwill among all the players of these great events now reigns. These two major historical events were the backdrop and setting that inspired this writer to write this historical fiction. This is a fiction written around actual and historical events that happened in Leyte and Samar, Philippines, and the states of Hawaii and California, USA from the 1930s to the present. All the characters, circumstances and plot were all created but set against actual historical events.

This is the story of our fictional characters, their loves, social conflicts, patriotism, economic struggles, triumphs and defeats set against the social and economic challenges during the post-Great Depression and pre-Civil Rights Movement periods in America, and the liberation of the Philippines and the Pacific during the Second World War. The fictional story and plot were deeply woven into the fabric of actual and major historical events that happened in Hawaii and California, USA and Leyte and Samar, Philippines. Any similarities to actual living and deceased persons in the story, although intended, is an exercise of literary license by the author and therefore should be treated purely as coincidence or fiction.

In Leyte, history repeats itself. It has many "Firsts" in history.

This is a paraphrase of the foreword of Francisco S. Tantuico, Jr.'s book, *Leyte, the Historic Islands.* Somehow the island of Leyte seems to figure prominently in a number of important past historical events in the Philippines. Leyte island is about 2,785 square miles in land area and the seventh largest island in the Philippine archipelago. It lies less than 600 kilometers southeast of the island of Luzon that form the "lower back" of what looks like a sitting dog that describes the archipelago. It connects with Samar island via the San Juanico Bridge and these two island provinces connect with the main islands of Luzon and Mindanao through the Maharlika Highway, the highway that starts from Northern Luzon down to Southern Mindanao. This highway was built in the 70s and was funded with the help of the Japanese government's Japan International Cooperation Agency (JICA). JICA is the Japanese counterpart of the United States Assistance for International Development (USAID). It coordinates all Japanese development assistance to developing countries like the Philippines.

These events are important and unique enough that it got the attention of the whole world because they were either firsts, or incomparable events that could only happen once in a lifetime. In addition, it changed the course of our modern history and the lives of a large group of people.

"Rediscovery of Leyte"

One of such events is the "rediscovery of Leyte" on March 16, 1521 by Ferdinand Magellan. Leyte is one of the 7,100 or so islands that comprise what we call now as the Philippine Archipelago. We put this under quotations to emphasize that this is contrary to what was written in history books by western historians that gave credit to Portuguese Ferdinand Magellan for the discovery of the Philippines. Research done by Zaide and Constantino, Filipino historians, and accounts of Figafetta, the historian who was with Ferdinand Magellan, are all in agreement that the Filipinos have been in touch with and were visited by other Asian and western Europeans long before Ferdinand Magellan strayed into Homonhon island to get fresh water.

From the large expanse of the Pacific Ocean, trade winds and ocean currents could naturally bring any sailboat to the shores of Samar and Leyte, just like what it did to Ferdinand Magellan's ships on March 16, 1521. This was a great historical event that changed the course and history of the Philippines, the only predominantly Christian country in Southeast Asia.

First Roman Catholic Mass at Limasawa Island

Then there was the celebration of the first Catholic mass in the Orient on March 31, 1521 at Limasawa island, just southeast of Leyte. The Philippines is preparing to celebrate 500 years of Catholicism on March 31, 2021 in commemoration of this event. Here historian Figafetta writes that the friendly natives led by a "Datu" with five wives ceremoniously welcomed in full regalia the Spanish invaders led by Magellan which led to the celebration of the first ever Roman Catholic mass in the Orient.

"The Battle of Leyte Gulf and the Leyte Landings"

Four hundred twenty-three years and eight months later, the Battle of Leyte Gulf, that started in October 23, 1944 and culminated on October 26, 1944 would happen as another major event military historians believe will never be duplicated in the future. This battle was between the American Third and Seventh Fleets and the mighty Imperial Japanese Navy. The Americans were defending and protecting the successful Leyte landings of the liberating forces under General MacArthur on the shores of Tacloban, Palo, Tolosa and Dulag, Leyte on October 20, 1944. The Japanese were set to destroy those landings and stop the liberation of the Philippines.

It was at Palo Leyte's "Red beach", that Gen. Douglas MacArthur uttered his famous words: *"People of the Philippines, I have returned. By the grace of Almighty God our forces are in Philippine soil again."*

According to military historians and writers, particularly Samuel Eliot Morison (Rear Admiral, Ret.) who wrote fifteen volumes of factual accounts of the history of the United States Naval Operations in World War II, the Battle of Leyte Gulf was considered as the greatest Naval Battle ever fought. In Volume 12 entitled "Leyte" (1963), he claims that this was principally because of three main reasons:

First, its impact on history and final outcome of the Second World War.

It led to the liberation of the Philippines, destruction of the mighty Imperial Japanese Navy (IJN) and eventual surrender of Japan;

Second, extent and geographic size of Battle.

The battle covered thousands of square miles (Leyte Gulf and South China Sea on the west, Formosa on the north, the boundary of Guam on the east and Sulu Sea on the South and Southwest); and

Third, the tonnage and strength of the forces involved.

The battle involved about 370 ships (large aircraft carriers, heavy and light Cruisers, battleships, and destroyers) from both sides, (US/Australia 300 versus Japan 67+) and more than 1,800 planes (US 1500, Japan 300+). Total navy personnel from both sides numbered more than 200,000. The logistical operation of transporting 20,000 tons of war materials, supplies and more than 160,000 troops within a couple of weeks was just unimaginable even at today's standards. Morison writes that nearly half of these were put on shore within only 72 hours. The operation was so large that it took the US Navy several months to report what happened at the Battle of the Leyte Gulf and the Leyte landings because the battle "had been too large, involved too many U.S. military personnel, ships and supplies, and had resulted in too much loss of life to ignore". It involved the last of the only two "battleship-to-battleship" shooting engagements during World War II. The first one was at the Battle of Guadalcanal. The naval battle at Guadalcanal involved only a fraction of the combined number of personnel, warships and airplanes from both sides that saw action at the Battle of Leyte Gulf. The Battle of Leyte Gulf involved on the one hand the whole force of the once mighty Imperial Japanese Navy (IJN) under the command of the Supreme Commander of the IJN, Admiral Toyoda. The armada included the heaviest and biggest battleships ever built, the Yamato and Musashi which had a combined displacement of 138,000 tons. On the opposing side of the battle involved the mighty US Third Fleet, the US Seventh Fleet, Australian warships, the US Sixth Army and the whole of the US Pacific Armed Forces, airmen and allies under the command of General Douglas MacArthur. The last and the bigger of the only two battleship-to-battleship gun duels of World War II happened at the Battle of Leyte Gulf.

Super Typhoon Haiyan (named Yolanda by the Philippine Atmospheric and Geologic Services Agency, PAGASA)

Super typhoon Haiyan was to date, the strongest Category 5 Tropical Cyclone ever recorded that made landfall. Category 5 cyclones are those that exceed 250 kilometers per hour wind in the center and are labelled as "catastrophic" in the scale of meteorologists. It made its first landfall in Guiuan, Eastern Samar and Tacloban City, Leyte at its maximum sustained wind speed of about 315 kilometers per hour or 195 miles per hour near the center. From Guiuan, it proceeded to wreak havoc in Tacloban City, Leyte leaving about 6,300 dead (official count) in its wake and the whole city of Tacloban completely destroyed and paralyzed. As a survivor of this cataclysmic event, this writer can vividly recount firsthand minute-by-minute, the passing of the great storm over Tacloban City, until all became quiet. Seven days after the storm, the stench of death enveloped the whole city as decomposing bodies that were still uncollected littered the main thoroughfares of the city. Only about 6,300 were reported as dead by the government because this number did not include the more than 20,000 that were missing. Missing bodies simply could not be legally counted as dead by government definition. In this writer's family alone two beloved septuagenarian aunts perished and their bodies were never found. Therefore, they were not counted as dead. One year after the November 8, 2013 deluge, bodies were still being discovered in the waters off the shores of Dulag, San Pedro Bay and San Juanico Strait and fresh skeletons of whole families were still being discovered under the debris that were being removed in hard hit Barangays of Tacloban City like San Jose and Magallanes. This writer could distinctly remember the sight of brown earth that were once verdant green hills and mountains and stumps of trees whose branches and leaves were completely blown away by the strong winds. One can picture a city blasted and blown away but not burned by fire.

Just like the historical events of Magellan's rediscovery of the Philippines, the first mass at Limasawa island, the Battle of Leyte Gulf, and the Leyte Landings, super typhoon Haiyan, although a natural cataclysmic event, also greatly impacted the rest of the world. It boosted the international concern for climate change. The storm's path of devastation were also the same historic places where our love story began, Eastern Samar and Leyte. It brought to the fore a story of untold suffering and devastation, but also the story of triumph and overcoming by a strong and resilient people, the people of Tacloban City and Guiuan, Eastern Samar.

We mention this natural event as another first in Leyte, because it also made a great historical impact on the Philippines and the rest of the world. People from all over the world, from all walks of life, the high and the mighty, the famous and not so famous came to Tacloban City and Guiuan to help ease the pain that the super typhoon caused. The International Red Cross, Red Crescent, USAID, UNCHR, Save the Children, Catholic Relief Services, Doctors Without Borders, Tzu Chi, Rotary International, Lions International, Jaycees International, among a hundred more charitable organizations pitched their tents in Tacloban City and Guiuan. Some stayed for more than a year, helping Tacloban City businesses recover by spending their money in the city.

Guiuan, Eastern Samar was home to the US Seventh Fleet in the Pacific before they had Clark Airbase in Angeles, Pampanga and the Subic Naval base in Olongapo City, located at the Bataan peninsula.

In addition to the US naval base and a US military airfield at municipalities of Mercedes and Guiuan, Eastern Samar that can handle C-130 cargo planes, the Pearl Island of Guiuan was also known for the "White Russian" settlement that once thrived there for two generations before they were distributed to different states in the US mainland in the 1950s. The "White Russians" were refugees who escaped from the Bolshevik revolution of communist Russia in 1918.

Their existence and temporary settlement in the Philippines however were only declassified in the fifties, after they were quietly repatriated to the US. The US naval base in Guiuan, Eastern Samar is nothing but thick vegetation now, but its long and well-maintained airfield is still being used from time to time, by the Philippine Armed Forces and the visiting US armed forces.

The lives of Filipino Immigrants to the US before, during and after the Great Depression and the Civil Rights movements in the US

Our story was also shaped and influenced by the actual events in the US before, during and after the Great Depression and the Civil Rights movement. Our setting were the pineapple and sugarcane fields in Hawaii and the farms and sweat shops in Central Valley, California. Before and during the hard struggle against discrimination by the African Americans in the Southeastern States of America, Filipinos were also discriminated against along with their African American brothers. The imperatives of the American involvement in the Second World War in the Pacific have created opportunities for African Americans and Filipinos to show what they can do for America. The difficult and delicate social and political issues brought about by segregated America ("*equal but separate*") did not exempt the US armed forces. Indeed, war brings both horror and opportunities. When General Douglas MacArthur decided to create a special brigade of Filipinos to be assigned to specific duties in the war effort and to his own staff, it changed the lives and fortunes of many Filipinos. It shaped the story of our main fictional characters.

Some Notes on Generation Classification

In our story, we speak freely of first, second, third and fourth generation Filipino-Americans to distinguish generations of Filipino immigrants who came to America at different time periods. Each group is defined according to the type of social, political, economic and even technological experiences each group was exposed to.

For example, the First-Generation Filipino-Americans were exposed to the difficult times of the Great Depression in America. These were times of great economic difficulty, unemployment and poverty, on top of segregation and racial discrimination. Then the Second-Generation Filipino-Americans had to deal and face up with one of the world's greatest disruptors, the Second World War. The Third-Generation Filipino-Americans had to deal with post war continuation of racial discrimination, inequality in the US and at the same time the rise and triumph of the Civil Rights Movement started by Martin Luther King. This movement broke major economic, social and political barriers in the American society that earlier prevented African Americans and ethnic minorities from advancing economically and politically. Television was the main technological disruptor for this generation of baby-boomers. The Fourth-Generation Filipino-Americans are now confronting their search for their own identity and place in the modern American pluralistic society. This is the result of their assimilation into mainstream American society, faster than they could handle. They are dealing with the positive and negative effects of the digital and electronic media, the internet and social media.

In terms of time periods, the First-generation Filipinos were the pioneers among Filipino Immigrants who came during the 1920s to the 1940s. This was the period when the Great Depression started and ended. Politically, the Philippines was just a colony of the United States of America.

The Second-generation Filipino immigrants where those who immigrated during and immediately after the war and after the Philippines became politically independent from the US (1941 to 1963).

The Third-generation Filipino-American immigrants where those who came during and after the Civil Rights movements broke ground and won more rights for all minorities in the US (1964 to 1996). Generation X and the Millennials were included in this generation by the Pew Research Foundation.

The Fourth-generation Filipino-American immigrants are the sons and daughters of Third-generation Filipino-American immigrants who have been assimilated into the mainstream American society. They were born after 1997, or the start of the Post-millennial generation. This was the period of political correctness, equal opportunity initiatives and the dismantling of social and political barriers to minorities in the US. This too was the period of the economic and political emancipation and empowerment of ethnic minorities particularly the Asians and Filipino-Americans.

We applied the tool developed by the US Census Bureau that distinguished and identified generations of Americans also according to social, political, economic and technological experiences common to each generation. The Census Bureau did this principally to distinguish the beginning and the end of the Baby-boomer generation. This was refined further by Michael Dimock, President of the Pew Research Center, a foundation engaged in gathering data to identify and analyze information about common experiences of each generation.

According to Dimock, the generation time periods is not an exact science but briefly they are as follows:

- The Silent Generation: Born 1928-1945 (73-90 years old)
- Baby Boomers: Born 1946-1964 (54-72 years old)
- Generation X: Born 1965-1980 (38-53 years old)
- Millennials: Born 1981-1996 (22-37 years old)

- Post-Millennials: Born 1997-Present (0-21 years old)

Set in this background of historical events in the US and the Philippines, our story begins, develops and climaxes to the present.

August 2, 2019

PROLOGUE

The people from India believe in "Kismet", a Sanskrit word meaning "fate". Filipinos call this "tadhana". Many of us Asians actually believe that at birth, we have a predetermined path of life. Asians are particularly open to this idea. They also believe that the position of celestial bodies in the universe affect their daily lives on earth. Astrology is therefore popular among Asians. This is because there are events that happen in our lives that could not easily be explained by conventional wisdom or even science.

Take for instance the lives of Macario Depuesto and Dalisay Borja. How does one explain how their two distinctly separate lives converged like it did during the liberation of Leyte from the Japanese occupiers? Both of their parents came from the same country though, the Philippines. The Depuestos originated from the Ilocos Region of northern Luzon while the Borjas were from Eastern Visayas. Macario originally came from the US mainland and was physically separated by the great Pacific Ocean before they met. They were about 10,000 miles apart from each other. We are reminded of a song that says that it is a wonder and a miracle how two people, separated by distance and location, circumstance and stations in life, find each other and fall in love. “In a world filled with strangers, how do two people find each other?”, says the song. To think that this was prior to the development of the internet as we know it, email and of course, Facebook, this was indeed very remarkable. Or again, call it fate, kismet or tadhana.

In the 1930s, Julian Depuesto (Macario’s father) came to America from the Ilocos Region of Northern Luzon in search of a better life for his family. This was during the end of the Great Depression when America was just starting to recover. What he found was not exactly what he was praying for because life then in the sugarcane fields of Hawaii was hard for immigrants or colored people. The economy, while it started to recover beginning in 1933, was still far from where it was before the 1929 crash.

It was worse in mainland USA from 1929 to 1933, during the height of the Great Depression. People lined up for food in the cities while farms in the Midwest became "dust bowls". People who had jobs lost up to 40% of their incomes while one out of four members of the labor force lost his/her job. Those who had money and had investments in the stock market lost 90% of their investments. Nearly half of the US banks failed. One could not think of any grimmer situation than this one.

When things got a little bit better in 1938, Macario's family decided to move to California from Hawaii for a better break and to escape the bondage of poverty and the lack of opportunities in the sugarcane fields. The Depuestos, along with nearly 200,000 others from all over America came to California, with nothing but hope and perhaps better expectations. However, what greeted them were the harsh realities of a segregated America and the height of discrimination against "colored" people. *But the course of history in the Philippines and the Pacific would dictate and shape Macario's future in America. To superstitious people this was his fate, his "kismet".*

Dalisay Borja on the other hand, lived all her young life in Dulag, Leyte, a sleepy fishing and farming town about 25 kilometers southeast of Tacloban City. Dulag's shorelines face the Pacific Ocean. A daughter of a poor fisherman and growing up as a teenager during the occupation by the Japanese of Dulag town, Dalisay had to live through very perilous if not extraordinary times. Instead of enjoying the carefree years of puberty and maidenhood, Dalisay had to skip adolescence and mature ahead of her age. By force of circumstances, she had to take responsibilities normally expected of people much older than her. But those times were different times, the Japanese occupation period of the Philippines.

Alas, Dalisay missed the lazy days of summer in her youth. This was too bad because Dulag was blessed with pristine waters in its beaches and rivers. Instead, she had to be a secret courier of the resistance movement against the Japanese, the Leyte guerillas. She had to endure and live in fear as she does her work for the guerillas instead of just worrying about what to do during warm summer days in Leyte. Under normal circumstances, girls of her age would only think about young boys, their crushes and their future or imagined prince charming. Not for Dalisay. This was wartime and life was cheap. Alive today but one could be dead tomorrow. Her life will forever change during and after the liberation of Leyte and a chance meeting with Macario Depuesto at the Palo Cathedral that was converted into an infirmary to take care of the wounded soldiers and civilians after the October 20 Leyte landings in 1944.

The Parallel Lives and Story of the Asis Family

Somewhere in the tobacco fields of Ilocos Norte, Manoling Asis was pondering on how he could make both ends meet as his wife Yolanda was heavy with their first child. He met Yolanda in a "tabacalera" near the old Port Area of Manila during one of their dried tobacco deliveries to the cigar and cigarette factory originally owned by some Spanish "caciques". Caciques are rich Spanish land owners who gained titles to their vast land through Royal grants from the King of Spain. They chose to stay in the Philippines even after the Americans took over the islands in December, 1898. Yolanda was a household help of the owner of the cigarette factory and was originally from what is now known as the town of Taft, Eastern Samar. At about the same time when Julian Depuesto received news that the American plantations in Hawaii were hiring hundreds of farm hands, Manoling also heard of the news. They grabbed the opportunity as well and took the first available boat for Oahu, Hawaii.

We do not really know if Manoling and Yolanda Asis boarded the same boat that carried Julian and Unding Depuesto and their toddler to Hawaii, but they both ended up in the sugarcane farms of Oahu, Hawaii. Economic circumstances would bring these two families in the farms of Oahu, Hawaii at about the same time, but they would only meet through their respective grandchildren Loreto Asis and Ligaya Depuesto in another place and during a much better time.

War Broke out in the Pacific; America Declares War Against Japan

On December 7, 1941, Sunday morning, unprovoked and without any warning, squadrons of Japanese torpedo and bomber planes from the carriers commanded by Admiral Yamamoto attacked Pearl Harbor in Hawaii. At about the same time, other squadrons of Japanese bombers destroyed the US bases in Clark airbase in Pampanga and the Nichols airfield in Manila. This led to the dramatic declaration of war against the Empire of Japan by President Franklin Delano Roosevelt before the joint session of the US Congress called for the purpose.

It would also change not only the course of history but also the lives, fate and fortunes of the Asis family, Depuestos and the family of Dalisay Borja.

CHAPTER 1

The Depuesto Family

"The Depuestos were poor. But they were ambitious, hardy and industrious."

Macario Depuesto was an above average Ilocano progeny. Standing at about 5 foot and 11 inches barefoot, his muscular build cuts an impressive figure among his fellow Filipino immigrants in the U.S. who originally came from the pineapple and sugarcane fields of Oahu, Hawaii. His fair complexion was much lighter than most Ilocanos who tended the fields under the burning heat of the sun. Judging from his aquiline nose, he probably inherited traces of Spanish genes from his Ilocano heritage from Sta. Maria, Ilocos Sur.

This Northern Luzon province called Ilocos Sur, and the town of Sta. Maria, his hometown, is home to a large Roman Catholic Basilica, set on top of a hill that gives a panoramic view of the town. Ilocos was a major enclave of the Spanish missionaries who came after Padre Pedro De Valderrama, one of the priests who accompanied Ferdinand Magellan in Limasawa Island. On that fateful and glorious summer day in the Philippines, on March 31, 1521, the first mass in the Orient was celebrated. The Roman Catholics in the Philippines will celebrate 500 years of Catholicism on March 31, 2021.

Macario missed the opportunity to grow up in this beautiful Ilocos town because, he was brought by his parents, Manong Julian and

Manang Unding to the island of Oahu, at an early age, to build a new life in the fertile valleys of the Hawaiian-islands. The demand for sugar in the US and the rest of the world has been growing and the American farmers strongly lobbied for the US government to allow farm workers from its colonies to immigrate and work in the US farms.

Then and even now, the American farmers belonged to the most powerful and influential group of lobbyists in the US. They were the same lobbyists who tried (in vain) to kill the Philippine coconut industry in 1935. They have not stopped trying really, ever since. But that is another story.

In 1933, a bunch of Manong Julian's fellow Ilocanos took the opportunity and boarded the first available boat that took them to the Hawaiian island of Oahu. A US government survey in the 1930s of about 38 plantations in Hawaii reported about 46,225 total farm workers in their payroll. Out of this total, 29,321 or 63.40% were Filipino workers!

The Depuestos were poor. But they were ambitious, hardy and industrious. It took a lot of courage for the father of Macario to immigrate to Hawaii, but compared to the hard life in the barren and smaller farms of Ilocos Sur, the fertile and volcanic land of Oahu seemed a lot more promising and a better option. Manong Julian and Manang Unding can barely read and write but they were literate enough to sign their names and count their money. They were among the hundreds of semi-literate and illiterate workers of the Hawaiian plantations.

Macario grew up among the Ilocano speaking farm workers in make-shift shanties at the pineapple and sugarcane fields. Their shanties or communities, if one can call them as such, were segregated from the settlement of whites and their families. The whites and the "colored" people did not mingle socially. Not even during worship. They only mingle at work because the whites were usually the foremen and supervisors that represent the owners of the farms. This was not the colored people's choice but rather this was how mainstream America was, before the Civil Rights Movement changed things, at least in principle.

In the 1920s, the California and Hawaiian Sugar Company (C and H Sugar Company) employed thousands of workers as a cooperative. The migrant plantation workers, like Julian Depuesto were not given membership in the cooperative. As profits grew and sugar demand in mainland USA expanded, the company provided for better tenement housing and benefits to its workers. This was not out of benevolence but rather out of necessity to hold and retain the badly needed farm workers in its sugarcane fields in Hawaii and Central Valley of California. At the very least, the improved housing provided a healthier environment where the workers can conserve their strength, be healthy and be productive. However, the company still paid them at “subsistence” level wages. For the workers, the improved housing conditions were good enough for them to stay. In addition, Macario’s dad and his fellow workers, had nothing to worry about as far as job security was concerned. The whites were not interested in taking their jobs that pay only less than 10 cents per hour in the 1930s. This may not seem much but compared to what Manong Julian makes at the farms in Ilocos, this was much better. They were the American version of the “sacadas” of the sugarcane fields of Negros and Iloilo Islands in the Philippines. They work for long hours under the Hawaiian sun using machetes and bolos to manually cut those canes to feed the ever-hungry sugar mills in Hawaii. But the job was good enough to feed the family of Manong Julian, Manang Unding and Macario. It gave them the opportunity to stay in America and for Macario to attend American public schools.

This was the period in America when women did not vote yet and long before Martin Luther King echoed his famous speech "I have a Dream". In Crockett and Carquinez, California where the Depuesto family eventually landed, "Negroes" (now replaced by the politically correct term African-Americans) and other "colored" people like Filipinos, were not able to patronize the same restaurants, public parks and toilets that the whites did. Hence it was not uncommon to see "No Filipinos and Dogs allowed" in certain restaurants and public places. "Colored" people were socially segregated from the white population. They only get to mingle socially with white people at work whenever the occasion calls for it. The better paying jobs are of course occupied by white people. The less-paying jobs were given to colored people, including Filipinos.

Thus, farm work and farm labor were almost the exclusive domain of colored immigrants like Filipinos. Other menial jobs that poorly pay like dishwashing, janitorial work, domestic help, laundry, etc. were reserved not only for Filipinos but also for other minorities like the Chinese, African Americans and Latinos.

The creation of the Special Filipino Brigade under General Douglas MacArthur

The love affair between General Douglas MacArthur and the Filipinos dated back when his own father, Lieutenant General Arthur MacArthur became Governor-General of the Philippines from 1900 to 1901. During his term, he sent expeditionary forces not only to quell pockets of rebellions but also to build roads and bridges in Samar, one of the islands in their newly acquired Philippine archipelago. Some of his former soldiers chose to stay in Samar and intermarried native women. To this day one will find American "mestizas and mestizos" in Northern and Eastern Samar where these soldiers were once deployed. Some even became successful entrepreneurs whose descendants are now among the respected families of both Samar and Leyte.

There had been many battles fought between the Filipino and American forces during the Filipino-American war from 1898 to 1902. After the mock battle between the Spaniards and George Dewey's fleet at Manila Bay on May 1, 1898, the Americans called these encounters with Filipino revolutionaries, mere insurrections. For Filipinos led by General Emilio Aguinaldo, these were part of their struggle for independence, but this time against the American invaders. In August 1898, the Filipino Revolutionary forces under Gen. Emilio Aguinaldo had surrounded the Spanish forces in Fort Santiago, Manila. Just as when the revolutionary forces were about to defeat the last remaining Spanish holdout in Manila, the American forces snatched the victory from the Filipinos. Earlier in Hongkong, Aguinaldo met with the Americans, including Commodore George Dewey to plot how to smuggle arms to Manila and overthrow the last remaining Spanish resistance in Manila with the cooperation of the Americans. The mock battle in Manila Bay was part of the scenario planned. The American soldiers under the command of Major General Wesley Merritt were therefore allowed by Aguinaldo to enter Manila and set up camp without having to fire a single shot. Instead, the Americans double-crossed Aguinaldo and took Manila for themselves. This precipitated the beginning of the Philippine-American war that ended in 1902.

The newly proclaimed Philippine republic from Malolos, Bulacan and later at Kawit, Cavite on June 12, 1898 signified that the Filipinos were already a sovereign nation, in the minds of Aguinaldo and his men. These were the events that preceded many encounters resulting in the massacre of Filipinos from December 1898 until the last Filipino holdout, General Vicente Lukban, surrendered in 1902 from the mountains of Leyte. The most infamous of these massacres was the slaughter of the inhabitants of Balangiga, Samar that included women and children ten years old and above after the so called "massacre" of 38 members of Company C of the US 9th Infantry Regiment that Gen.

Robert P. Hughes, commander of the Department of Visayas assigned to Samar. The brutal retaliation ordered by Brigadier General Jacob H. Smith was as follows:

"I want no prisoners. I wish you to kill and burn; the more you kill and burn, the better it will please me... The interior of Samar must be made a howling wilderness."

No accurate number of the Samar population slaughtered by the American soldiers was ever reported but some American and Filipino historians believe that up to 50,000 may have been killed. This was what happened after General Arthur MacArthur was replaced as Governor General. He caught part of the Philippine-American war, particularly in the pacification of Samar and Leyte. At that time, the Philippines was governed by the Americans through a Governor General, just like their Spanish predecessors. One of whom would become President of the United States of America, William Howard Taft.

The growing importance of the Philippines to America since they took over the islands in 1898 from its former Spanish colonial masters was driven by two things: its location as the farthest forward colony of the US in Southeast Asia where they could have military bases; and second, the growing threat of Communism after the Second World War. The strategic importance and location of the Philippines would grow even more during the height of the Cold War between Communist Soviet Russia and Communist China on one hand and the U.S. and the rest of the "free world" on the other.

A post or assignment in Manila was therefore coveted by ambitious American bureaucrats or military officials. Some of the famous generals of the Second World War, would therefore have tours of duty in the Philippines during the Philippine Commonwealth period before the outbreak of the Pacific war. Among them were then Colonels Dwight Eisenhower and Douglas MacArthur.

The move to California, A leap of Faith

Growing up under the harsh and challenging conditions of farm work in Hawaii, Macario had been struggling to adjust to the American way of life in the mainland. In California, where there were other jobs aside from farm work at the Central Valley after the Great Depression of 1930s, Macario began to see the stark differences between white America and colored America. A hard life was not new to Macario. He knew how it was to be poor and to struggle for daily survival at the farms. But the situation in California, and for that matter mainland America was more difficult to comprehend for young Macario. He saw the great divide between white America and colored America. In California he saw how affluent some communities appear to be and how different they were compared to where he lived. It was hard enough for a teenager to deal with puberty and changes in his body, but more so if one had to make sense of the life and the society they had to reckon with and assimilate. An indelible image of the American society began to form in Macario's adolescent mind. America is the land of plenty but only if you are white.

Macario was handsome and tall by Asian standard. Like any handsome adolescent, Macario would have a few crushes and a few girls of his age would likewise take interest in him. But they were usually white teenagers. This was a big problem at that time. Without being told by his parents, Macario knew where he stood and where his boundaries were. Mixed-race dating was simply taboo during those years of adolescence of Macario. He therefore could not and did not get into a serious or long-term relationship with any particular opposite sex in California. But growing up, he experienced his own share of the youthful “rites of summer” in sunny and warm California.

Manong Julian also tried his hand in different jobs that establishments were willing to hire him for. Being ambitious, he wanted a better paying job, one that pays more than 10 cents an hour. This desire took him away from the vegetable farms of California’s Central Valley where manual labor jobs were always abundant. He ended up in Port Chicago, City of Martinez, Northern California. This is a few miles southeast of Sacramento, the present capital of the “sunshine” State. He and his son Macario, eventually got a job in the ammunition factory and depot of the US Armed Forces at Port

Chicago, Martinez where they manufactured explosives and ammunition for the US Navy and the Armed Forces. Of course, the job at the ammunition factory and the loading of these munitions and explosives were among the most dangerous jobs there was. The "white masters" were just too willing to give it to Manong Julian, Macario and the "Negroes".

"Heck, if I am going to die, better to die with a little more money in my pocket than none at all," Julian said to himself when he submitted his application. There was no hesitation on the part of Manong Julian. He took the job at the explosives plant along with a bunch of African Americans who were willing to take the risk.

Then fortunately or unfortunately, war broke out in the Pacific and the demand for munitions and explosives suddenly skyrocketed. The Martinez facility became a major military installation that supported the American war effort. It became a fertile hunting ground for the recruitment of special units that would perform special assignments for the US Armed Forces. The US Armed Forces created special units as one of the ways to deal with segregation issues.

For this reason, in 1943 Gen. Douglas MacArthur created a special unit, a whole brigade of African Americans that will be trained and deployed to different stations and theatres of the war. In addition, because of MacArthur's affinity for Filipinos and his promise to return to the Philippines after he escaped from Corregidor via submarine to Australia in March 11,1942, he also created a special brigade composed of Filipinos with special assignments and duties to perform for him as Commander of the US Armed Forces in the Far East (USAFFE).

Fliers and notices about the recruitment were circulated in areas like Hawaii and California where there were many Filipinos.

"Uncle Sam needs you. Join the navy!" says the flier. This did not escape eighteen-year-old Macario's curious eyes.

"Perhaps see the world too?", he said to himself. He was one of the curious if not the more adventurous volunteers from the ranks of Filipinos. In Port Chicago alone, the lines were long. Perhaps the lines were longer in Honolulu, Hawaii.

For sure it was not about patriotism or love of Uncle Sam that drew a lot of these Filipinos to answer the call. It was something else. For Macario, anything better than the Port Chicago job was good enough. Besides, he was ready for the next adventure of his life.

"Many are called but only few are chosen"

Of the more than four-thousand who responded, less than a third were called for the interview. Then there were just 900 of them for the final screening and physical examination. Of these finalists, only 400 were selected with a hundred more on stand-by, just in case some of the finalists cannot assume the assignment. For one thing the physical requirements were tough. One has to be physically fit, must be at least 5' 5" in height, can read and write in English and must be of Filipino parentage.

Many actually failed in the literacy requirement. Many of these Filipino farm hands could barely read and write. The height requirement was also reduced by one inch to accommodate some good prospects. Macario passed all these first stage screening. Thanks to his fascination to Carlos Bulusan's literature, his good reading abilities although mostly self-taught, helped him through. This was how he occupied his nights when most young men his age would spend time dating or doing what young virile men and women would do in the California levies.

At the final interview, Macario did very well. His good looks and charm did the rest. Being one among the few chosen in a field of more than 4,000 applicants was a very respectable feat. He trained hard and somehow ended up doing physical therapy at the Medical Unit of the Filipino brigade. This work was similar to that of a midwife and a physical therapist. It required a thorough mastery of the human body and techniques in the application of first aid.

Soon after, Gen. MacArthur himself met and exhorted the graduating batch of the Filipino Brigade before they were dispatched to their specific assignments. He immediately took notice and a liking for young Macario, as he stood tall among the other successful Filipino members of the brigade. Among other duties, Mac as he will later be called by the general, became a personal physical therapist of Gen. Douglas MacArthur. He was promoted as First Class private immediately. After a few more training, he would be promoted as Staff Sergeant, assigned to the exclusive "cordon sanitaire" of the General. Having reached this level of association with and working at close physical proximity to General Douglas MacArthur, Macario had to pass several military security clearance screenings. He passed them all in flying colors. At that time, no other Filipino of his humble stature possessed the military security clearance he was given.

This is the beginning our story that will unfold throughout the course of the Pacific War and the liberation of the Philippines. Macario Depuesto, single and approaching the prime of his age and career was among the immediate aide-de-camp of Gen. Douglas MacArthur, the Supreme Commander of the USAFFE, in command of American and Allied forces at the Pacific theatre of the war. On July 17, 1944, at the height of the frenzy to load ammunitions and explosives to naval ships bound for the Pacific theatre, a huge explosion at Port Chicago, Martinez occurred killing 320 sailors and civilians and injuring 390 others. Most of the dead and injured were of course enlisted African American sailors and civilians. Macario would have probably been among those dead or injured if not for the new assignment he got from Gen. MacArthur.

This was part of his "kismet". He was meant to live and play a role in the liberation of the Philippines.

Chapter 2

The Asis Family

"...they were not particularly religious, but they were upright and God-fearing Ilocanos whose only fault was that they were poor and they belonged to the margins of Philippine society."

From the tobacco farms of Ilocos to the sugarcane farms of Hawaii

Loreto Asis was the grandson of Manoling Asis, a tobacco farmer from Pagudpud, Ilocos Norte and Yolanda Cinco from what is now known as the municipality of Taft, a coastal town in Eastern Samar facing the Pacific Ocean. Loreto's father, Arnulfo was born in the ghettoes of Oahu sugarcane plantation and spent his childhood in Hawaii. Loreto was born in Vallejo, California from the union of Arnulfo Asis with an Italian-American, Simona Niones. The dominant genes of the Asis showed in Loreto's physical appearance. Stocky, brown in complexion and five foot six inches in height. Except for the long eyelashes and his twangy American accent, he looked every bit an Asian. A Filipino, one might even say. He inherited a lot of his grandparents and his father's physical attributes. But in terms of thinking, attitude and habits, Loreto was very much an American. He is brown in complexion but thinks, acts and talks like any white American. Born after the war and raised by a middleclass family based on the prevailing social and economic standards then, Loreto grew up as a confident, precocious American teenager with a lot of great expectations for his future. Unlike his grandparents and parents who first had to struggle for their survival in the farms all the way to Vallejo California, Loreto had a fairly normal and comfortable life raised from a family that enjoyed the perks and retirement benefits of a US army war veteran. His mother Simona likewise came from a middleclass Italian-American family. She likewise had educational benefits arising from the military service of her father. She took advantage of these benefits when it was time for her to go to college.

Manong Manoling and Manang Yolanda, Arnulfo's parents were not very literate although they could numerate. They did not learn to read and write until much later in life when Arnulfo himself started attending grammar school for the children of plantation workers in Oahu, Hawaii. At age 8, Arnulfo would get his first book of American Grammar and would attend a grammar school run by volunteers from a Christian Baptist church. This was part of their evangelization so that they would be able to own and read their own bibles.

The Asises were baptized Catholics in the Philippines but owing to the distance of the main Catholic churches (which were in Paoay and Laoag, Ilocos Norte) from where they lived, they did not attend Sunday masses regularly. They received some catechism classes from the Jesuits and the Dominican missionaries who would occasionally come by their barrio in Pagudpud. For this reason, one might say that they were not particularly religious, but they were upright and God-fearing Ilocanos whose only fault was that they were poor and they belonged to the margins of Philippine society.

Arnulfo, just like his father Manoling, was stocky and heavy set and muscular that was ideal for manual labor. Although Arnulfo's complexion was brown, he and his father were on the darker shade of brown as both have been working under the heat of the sun for the most part of the day at the sugarcane fields. He had to be fitted with prescription glasses at an early age when he started school. His father Manoling might have had the same problem but they never had to use a pair of glasses because neither of them had to read much anyway. The discovery of Arnulfo's problem with his eye-sight came about in a round-about way. The first few weeks after Arnulfo started his grammar school, his teacher noticed that while being attentive and always on task, he would not do well in written quizzes. He would fail almost all his quizzes although he did not miss a day in class. He would also respond well during recitations.

One day Arnulfo's teacher would ask his father for a private counseling session at his office. On the way to the teacher's office, Manoling was already scolding him and warned him that he will whip him with his "yantok mindoro" if he finds out what kind of trouble his son was in. "Yantok mindoro" is a stick made from rattan that grew abundantly in the virgin forests of the Philippines. The ones that grew in the Mindoro island was preferred for its quality and maximum pliability. Rattan is an important Philippine forest product that is now fast disappearing. It is used by skilled furniture makers for making the beautiful rattan furniture that is still being exported to America today. Mindoro is an island southwest off Batangas and the Bataan peninsula. A rattan cane is about one to one and a half inches in diameter, and about two and a half to three feet long. It is very deadly when used as a whipping stick. During those days, it was a highly feared household gadget that was usually used to "discipline" misbehaving children among Filipino households. Arnulfo was asked to seat on a chair outside the door as Manoling was led into the room by Mr. Smith, the American grammar teacher and missionary.

"What seems to be the problem?" Manoling anxiously asked Mr. Smith as soon as he was seated. "Is my son giving you problems?"

"Not at all but we hope it is nothing serious that is why I need to ask you a few questions," Mr. Smith replied.

"Well, that is why I am here sir," Manoling responded with some air of irritation. This attitude of Manoling stems from his dislike from dealing with whites like Mr. Smith. Although Mr. Smith was a kind missionary who belonged to that sector in the American society who believed in the fair, if not equal treatment of colored people, Manoling still did not trust him. He has had enough of the condescending ways of most whites when they talk to his kind, especially in the plantation.

"How is your family? Is everything ok with you, and your wife?" Mr. Smith continued, as if to break the tension that was building up.

Now looking really puzzled and surprised, Manoling replied, "We are ok sir. We eat three times a day, get to sleep more than five hours a day and we were told that we will have better housing next month."

"I will go straight to the point Mr. Asis. Arnulfo has failed all his written quizzes last week and he seems to be having problems keeping notes. He is falling behind in his grammar lessons" said Mr. Smith. "I am just puzzled because I know he is a very smart boy, never missed a class, very attentive and recites well. His failing in his quizzes is a mystery to me," continued Mr. Smith.

"Well, my guess is as good as yours Mr. Smith. Yolanda talks to him everyday and I have not heard of anything unusual about him, not even a complaint from the boy himself Sir," he politely replied.

"I just want to rule out any possible emotional situation in your household because I know he can do better and I want to know how to help him, with your support as parents" Mr. Smith assured Manoling.

"Why don't we ask him directly then. He is waiting outside," Manoling suggested.

Arnulfo by now was perspiring profusely and really anxious of what was transpiring between his father and Mr. Smith. Finally, he was let in and was seated beside his father, directly facing Mr. Smith.

"Arnulfo, what is wrong with you? You are falling behind and you have been failing in class," Manoling admonished his son, looking at him with accusing eyes.

"Whoa, hold your horses sir, we just want to ask Arnulfo here if he has been experiencing any problems since he failed his most recent quizzes, but he is not totally failing at all, Mr. Asis," Mr. Smith quickly reassured Manoling.

After a short pause, Arnulfo slowly raised his head because he was bowed down all this time during the exchanges between his father and Mr. Smith.

"I have been having headaches lately but only when I try to read what is written on the blackboard and our grammar textbook. I could not really take notes and could not concentrate. I also could not do my homework because I get headaches and sometimes it is so bad, I feel like throwing up," Arnulfo explained while glancing once in a while sideways to his unhappy father.

"I think, I know now what is the problem!" Mr. Smith happily declared as if he was one of those gold miners who discovered gold in northern California.

"We have to send him to an eye doctor," continued Mr. Smith.

With this Manoling raised his eyebrows but before he could utter a word, Mr. Smith put his index fingers perpendicular to his lips, as if to silence him and said, "Do not say a word, we will take care of the medical expenses."

"Will you allow your son to go with me to see an eye doctor?" asked Mr. Smith.

"Well, I suppose it is fine with me and Yolanda. We really could not afford it though, for sure. I myself have never seen an eye doctor in my life. But if you think this is necessary to help our boy in his studies, I should thank you in advance," Manoling meekly replied to the generous offer of Mr. Smith.

The following week, Arnulfo was brought to an eye doctor. This doctor attends the same church as the Smiths' and usually donates his time and services to the congregation's charitable undertakings. The doctor prescribed a reading glass for Arnulfo, the cost of which was paid for by donations from the church while the services of the doctor was free. This was how some members of mainstream American society mitigate the abuses and racial discrimination perpetuated by their fellow white Americans against colored people.

The Move to Vallejo, California

The Asis family, eventually migrated to California just as when Arnulfo was entering 12th grade. Manoling found work in

California's Central Valley and lived in Fresno during the war years. Arnulfo for sure also heard of the call for Filipinos to join a special unit of the US Armed Forces but he did not even bother to apply. In fact, he ignored it because he was born in Hawaii and is therefore a natural born American, not a Filipino. But like the older Depuestos, Arnulfo would witness the racial discrimination that all colored people, including Filipinos and Chinese were subjected to. Because of his complexion, he too was barred from entering establishments through the front door. He could protest if he was subjected to the same indignities Filipinos were subjected to and would probably be treated better (not equal) as a natural born Hawaiian native, but he would rather avoid the inconvenience. He would play it safe and avoid possible confrontation by keeping to himself and his immediate Italian-American friends and family.

In California, hordes of Latinos would come up to California from Mexico. After all, California was once part of Mexico, until the Americans expanded westward in 1849, all the way to the Pacific coast of California.

Unlike in the Hawaiian-islands, whose natives were Hawaiians and Samoans, the Latinos outnumbered all other ethnic minorities working in the Central Valley. California did not have an abundant supply of manual laborers so the farms depended heavily on these migrant workers. In fact, the real natives of California were American Indians and those who came from Mexico. When the Americans opened up the West for settlement by the whites, they had to rely on American Indians and migrants from Mexico to build their settlements. In the 15th and 16th centuries, the Spaniards with the help of Spanish colonizers and missionaries conquered and Christianized the natives of California.

They built missions connected by roads called "Caminos" from the south going up all the way to Northern California. This long highway that went from southern to northern California was called "El Camino Real". The missions that lined El Camino Real started and built the plantations of the fertile Central Valley of California. Naturally, these farms would grow and will become the vegetable and fruit baskets of America.

California would draw the natives of Mexico and of course Hawaii and the Chinese as population grew in the US mainland. California farms were relied upon by the rest of America to supply the population with vegetables, fruits and even livestock. When the Americans built the railroads from the east to the west and southwest, they attracted all, African Americans, Chinese, the Latinos and Filipinos from Hawaii. California and the southwest therefore became a melting pot of ethnic minorities namely the Latinos, the African Americans, Chinese, Pacific Islanders and Filipinos. Unlike in Hawaii, Arnulfo and his fellow Hawaiians and Ilocanos from Hawaii were outnumbered by the Latinos in California.

Arnulfo therefore would stay out of trouble with his Latino co-workers but will not hesitate to mix it up with them when provoked. His stocky build, large biceps and big sturdy thighs were enough to intimidate anyone, let alone his attitude. He too was acting like a racist and disliked any association with the Latinos and even the African Americans who would stray in the farms every now and then. He just wanted to protect his own space. Arnulfo was a survivor and this was how he protected himself from getting hurt or abused in the not-so-gentle world of farm workers. One had to be tough or show toughness in order to survive and be respected in the farms.

When the war broke out, Arnulfo, just like other Americans had to answer the draft and was sent to the European theatre of the war. We will hear again about him and his family at the end of the war.

After D-Day on June 6, 1944, the war was practically coming to an end in Europe. From the beaches of Normandy, France, the Allied Forces rapidly drove deep into Europe and engaged the Russians in a race towards Berlin, Germany. The Russians were coming from the North, while the Americans were driving up from the south to the finish line, the gates of Brandenburg, Germany.

By May 8, 1945, Germany capitulated.

Chapter 3

Preparations for the Leyte Landing and the Battle of Leyte Gulf

"MacArthur has to keep his promise. He was going to do it even if it kills him!"

One crisp and nippy evening of March, 1944, in his quarters at Washington D.C., Gen. MacArthur retired early, haggard and tired from an acrimonious meeting with the

Defense Secretary, other top aides of President Roosevelt and the other members of the Joint Chiefs-of-Staff. Earlier that day, MacArthur was not only grappling with the heavy burden of how to win the Pacific War against the mighty Japanese Imperial Navy (JIN) but he was also struggling with the prospect of the Philippines being by-passed by the US liberation forces in the Pacific. This was the common sentiment of the other commanders, Admirals Nimitz and King, including Gen. Dwight Eisenhower who wanted to by-pass the Philippines and proceed directly to Formosa, Taiwan prior to a possible invasion of Japan.

In the mind of the General, this was not acceptable, considering his promise to the Filipino people. He had been too public in his promise to return to the Philippines, especially at a speech he delivered in Australia upon his escape from Corregidor.

MacArthur has to keep his promise. He was going to do it even if it kills him!

“Mac, I need you now, pronto!” the general exclaimed as he called on his loyal Filipino physical therapist.

"Sir, yes sir!" was the familiar but snappy reply by Mac as he came up ready with his prized coconut oil and some mentholated balm in hand. He promptly helped the General to lie face down and on his stomach at the massage table. He started massaging the aching body of the General.

More than the muscles that hurt, Gen. MacArthur was aching deep inside in the prospect of not being able to keep his promise to his beloved Filipinos. Macario could sense and feel the agony his superior was in as he gently kneaded his back muscles. With every kneading stroke of the General's shoulder and back muscles, Macario could feel the general's pain, but he was just too intimidated by him or too afraid to ask what was the matter. Quietly but surely, Macario just continued to do his work, gently easing those tired and stressed muscles until the general fell asleep.

The following morning, the general was up early, took a shower, put on his favorite khaki shirt and trousers and was ready for coffee and toast. He called Mac to his breakfast table as he took a final sip of his coffee.

"Mac, thank you for your kind service last night. I know that what I want to accomplish today is also important to you. I will try again. If you want to see your folks in Ilocos Sur sooner than later, you better pray for me to get things done today," exclaimed the General.

Not really knowing the head or tail of this short conversation, Macario snappily replied, "Sir yes sir! I will pray to the Sto. Nino and ask for the intercession of the Blessed Virgin Mary for you sir."

"Good", MacArthur snappily retorted as he put his cap on, his Ray-Ban and went for the door to his waiting service car.

Admirals Ernest J. King and Chester W. Nimitz Strategy

The atmosphere was tense but the members of the Joint Chiefs-of-Staff were cordial if not polite. They all agreed that to force the unconditional surrender of Japan, the Allies must obtain and control bases from where to launch a massive invasion force. The question was which and where should these bases be? Admirals King and Nimitz were of the belief that the attack should be launched from Formosa and the Chinese coastlines that lie on the door steps of Japan. To do this, it would require the control of the mostly uninhabited Bonin islands, located south of Tokyo and parts of the coasts of China to launch the main attack from Formosa. This meant that the Philippines had to be by-passed. But General MacArthur on the other hand strongly believed that the "New Guinea and Mindanao Axis" approach that requires the liberation of the Philippines from south to north was the best route to a successful invasion of Japan. But King warned that "battering our way to the Philippines" would be a long and costly process. Both Nimitz and King further argued that their bold and more direct strategy would bring the defeat of Japan nearer. The two also thought that by-passing their loyal allies in the Philippines would not cause real hardship on their Philippine friends.

But the Japanese made two moves that helped MacArthur's plan gain the upper hand. First, the Japanese moved their main naval fleet from inland Japan to Linga Road in Singapore. The reason for this was that they wanted to be nearer their source of fuel oil. The second Japanese move that made MacArthur's plan better was when they moved their army to Canton, China, forcing out the XIV US Army from the forward airfields in China and cutting off Chiang Kai-shek out of the Chinese mainland. This ruled out any possibility of landing on friendly Chinese shores, as initially assumed by Nimitz and King.

At their next Command meeting in London, shortly after the Normandy D-Day, in June 1944, MacArthur was outraged that King and Nimitz still assumed that their "By-pass the Philippines for Formosa strategy" was still the preferred choice! MacArthur at this point delivered his impassioned plea to honor his (and America's) word to Filipinos to liberate them from Japanese tyranny at the earliest possible time. He eloquently argued that there was nothing good to gain from by-passing the Philippines, logistically or otherwise. He warned of the dire consequences of leaving the archipelago with its 16,000,000 loyal population to "wither in the vine" until Japan was defeated. Doing so was wrong and will cause "untold hardship to Filipinos and the rest of Asia will lose faith in American honor."

And so, it came to pass that in July, 1944, late as it was, in the presence of President Roosevelt and the Joint Chiefs-of-Staff, Gen. Douglas MacArthur got the final nod of everyone to liberate the Philippines first via Mindanao or the Visayas, instead of Formosa. The General's passionate speech, one that only Gen. Douglas MacArthur could deliver, turned resistance into full support to make his famous promise to the Filipinos, *"I shall return"* a reality.

Intelligence Couriers

Meanwhile in the hills of Mahaplag in what is now known as Southern Leyte, a group of Filipino resistance fighters under the command of a charismatic and highly respected leader named Ruperto Kangleon, were busy consolidating the intelligence information that was passed on to them by their colleagues operating in Leyte, and Samar. These encrypted messages were received from American submarines who periodically surface in undisclosed spots in northern Mindanao, Cebu and Guiuan,

Eastern Samar. One of these submarines was the Nautilus, the first nuclear powered submarine of the US Navy. In one of its sorties into the Philippine Seas in late in July 1944, it brought the top-secret liberation plan that was approved by the Joint Chiefs-of-Staff, Secretary Marshall and General Douglas MacArthur. Nautilus surfaced in San Roque, a coastal barrio of Abuyog town, southern part of Leyte island. It was Col. Ruperto Kanleon's group that received the top-secret messages from General Douglas MacArthur.

During this time, prior to the Leyte landing, there were different groups of guerillas operating in the Leyte island. Each group operated independently and were led by their own commanders who would not be answerable to anyone but the Americans only. Naturally each group competed with each other to gain the attention and respect by the Americans. Unfortunately, some of these rivalries resulted in unnecessary loss of lives between guerilla units when rivalry degenerated to firefights. In spite of these rivalries with other units, Col. Ruperto Kangleon managed to distinguish himself to the Americans above the others because of his well-executed plans and operations. His reliability as a leader of a cohesive group plus the quality of intelligence information that General MacArthur received from him made him stand out and the guerilla unit of choice by MacArthur. The messages his group received in San Roque from the Nautilus were to be disseminated to the different guerilla units operating in Luzon, Visayas and Mindanao. The purpose was to coordinate the pre-landing operations required by the US landing forces such as intelligence gathering on the strength, location of major Japanese camps and defenders. The latest intelligence information was to synchronize all operations towards ensuring the success of the planned landings in October and to confirm the exact site of the landings in Leyte.

Colonel Kangleon became particularly anxious and under stress in view of the delicate role they would play. Afterall, the landings will be in their area of operations, the Leyte eastern coasts. All the information that they would relay back to the fast-approaching American forces had to be fresh and accurate. Any change of plans that will significantly have a bearing on the planned landings have to be telegraphed without delay to the Americans. Luis Borja was assigned as one of these intel information couriers whose areas of responsibility included Tacloban, Dulag, Burawen, Kanangga and Ormoc. These were the areas where major Japanese camps and garrisons were located. The most important among these was Ormoc where Yamashita set up his last line of defense and was the chosen exit point for the general just in case the Japanese defense were not able to stop and confine the American forces in Palo, Leyte.

The truth was, as late as the month of July, General Yamashita and his superiors in Tokyo did not think that the Americans would land in Leyte. Not during the monsoon and typhoon months of July to October. The Japanese believed that November would be pushing their luck too much and the most rational choice would therefore be January to March of the following year. Hence, Yamashita, saved for its regular troops already stationed in Leyte and Mindanao, saw no need to reinforce or defend Leyte and Mindanao. At best, Yamashita wanted to delay the American advance to Luzon if they did land in Leyte and at the same time fight them to exhaustion so that the “invaders” will not be so fresh and strong when they proceed to Luzon.

But to win a war, like in a game of chess, one must not be predictable and must make moves not foreseen or expected by one’s opponent. The element of surprise was very important and moves that puzzle the opponent were best if only to confuse and hide intentions. Besides, in terms of numbers and logistics, the Japanese forces in the Philippines were no longer as formidable as the American forces that would pour on the shores of Leyte. The Japanese Imperial Armed Forces had been too spread out from the Malayan peninsula, Borneo and the South Pacific in addition to their fast dwindling resources and manpower. General Douglas MacArthur left Corregidor in 1942 in a PT boat. He would come back to Leyte two and a half years later with “the greatest naval armada the world would ever see.”

Finalizing the Leyte landing plan

Onboard USS Nashville, General MacArthur’s command ship, just a few nautical miles off Leyte Gulf, the General gathered his war-operations staff at the ship's war-room in the evening of October 17, 1944 to make a last-minute briefing about the landing that is supposed to happen after a massive bombardment or "softening" of the Leyte shores. They were to bombard the beaches of Leyte from Tacloban to Dulag, the length of which is almost 12 kilometers. Intelligence reports were therefore important at this time to confirm and pin point where the Japanese guns and pockets of resistance were located and to avoid or minimize civilian casualties from the bombardment of the beaches. They color-coded the beaches where they would land. General MacArthur's party will land on "Red Beach", the code name for the Palo, Leyte beach.

Meanwhile, at this very night, somewhere near the shores of Dulag, Leyte, Dalisay Borja was still grieving upon hearing of the news that her good friend, benefactor and secret lover, Captain Yamaguchi, was assassinated and killed at the supposed meeting she helped arrange.

Three months earlier, Admiral William Halsey, the commander of the mighty US 3rd

Fleet, made lightning raids in Luzon, Leyte and some parts of Mindanao using B-17 bombers to gauge the strength of Japanese resistance from these areas. They wanted to confirm if the planned Leyte Landing was a good choice. Gen. Halsey was pleasantly surprised at the lack of heavy resistance from the Japanese, especially during the Leyte raids. The results of the bombing raids indicated that Japanese resistance from their raids were minimal, at least in Leyte and parts of Mindanao. This reinforced further their plan to land in Leyte instead of Mindanao. KING TWO was on schedule for the October 20, 1944 landing at Leyte, Philippines.

CHAPTER 4

The Borjas and the Little Tokyo of Dulag, Leyte

"Do this for your country and your people, not me!"

The coastal town of Dulag, Leyte was a thriving fishing and farming town before the

Japanese came and occupied Leyte in 1942. Mano Berto and Mana Teresa Borja lived right at the edge of the beach, just at the foot of Catmon Hill, the highest point in Dulag that affords a panoramic view of the Leyte Gulf. On this hill, rising about 1,000 feet above sea level, an American flag used to fly on a flagstaff before the Japanese set up its own military encampment on top of the hill. The American flag was unceremoniously replaced by the rising sun flag of the Japanese.

Mano Berto and Mana Teresa were blessed with a son named Luis and a daughter named Dalisay. Just barely 18-years old, Luis went to the hills to join the guerillas, as soon as the Japanese set foot in Tacloban, Leyte. His younger sister Dalisay stayed behind to help her mother with household chores while Mano Berto went fishing. She was just fifteen years old when the Japanese invaded the Philippines and when Bataan fell on April 9, 1942. Like many teenagers of her age, she too missed the carefree years of adolescence and was forced to deal with the dangers of living in a Japanese occupied country. The fear of being raped was real as many horror stories of rape and torture quickly traveled from the Japanese garrisons of San Jose Del Monte, Bulacan and occupied Manila.

The Borja family therefore had every reason to protect and conceal Dalisay from the Japanese, who at sixteen was like a flower who is nearing its full bloom. In addition, they had to hide the fact that they have a son who joined the guerillas in the hills of Leyte and Samar. Since Luis left for the hills to join the guerillas, their contact with him had been few and far in-between. They hear about him only when someone from the guerilla units came down to Dulag to gather intelligence information from their assets in Dulag and from Mano Berto. From Luis, the guerillas learned that the family had access to the Japanese garrison.

The men had to do this secretly, behind the backs of Mana Teresa and Dalisay. This matter was left to the men in the family only. The women were not really consulted about what was going on in the resistance movement. Through Mano Berto, the guerillas were fed with the strategic information needed by the guerillas like the movements of the troops from Dulag, their strength and whenever possible, their plans. They were also fed with the lay-out and map of the whole garrison, taking note of the most secure and heavily guarded sections of the garrison.

As much as possible, they would not let Dalisay go out in public for fear of being noticed or seen by the Japanese soldiers. If ever she had to go, she would be with her mother. She would be completely covered by a large "salakot" (a wide-rimmed hat made from buri or palm leaves) and draped with "tapis" from head to toe. Her hair would be pulled back and tied into a tight bun and will only be untied to fall gracefully to her back and shoulders when she was at home. Tapis is a very colorful, long rectangular native cloth made from fine abaca fiber. It is much finer than the abaca jute sack. This is commonly worn by women in the non-Muslim areas of the Philippines. It is similar to the Muslim "malong" but different because the malong ends are sewn together to form a loose tubular sack open at both ends. The tapis is just a flat rectangular sheet of cloth and is usually wrapped around the body of the person wearing it. Dalisay's face could hardly be seen under the salakot while her upper body and arms are adequately covered by long sleeved blouses. She used a pair of "bakya" (wooden shoes) that will only show her toe nails and her ankles when she walks to the town with her mother. In December of 1942, a garrison was set up in Dulag that served as both a Japanese military camp and a detention center.

Major Inoue, a stocky and a fearsome officer in his forties established the garrison using forced labor from the people of Dulag and from prisoners taken from nearby municipalities of Tacloban and Ormoc. There were very few prisoners from Dulag town itself. By April of 1943, Major Inoue the first commander of the garrison was called and re-assigned by General Tomoyuki Yamashita for another assignment in Mindanao. At that time, General Tomoyuki Yamashita was the over-all commander of all the land based Japanese armed forces in the Philippines.

The local town breathed with a sigh of relief upon Inoue's re-assignment and departure. Still there was much anxiety because nobody knew if his replacement would be better or worse. By this time, the Japanese military intelligence gathered that the Americans and its allies will try to liberate the Philippines but they could not confirm where or when they would land. They just had not guessed exactly when or where the Americans would do it but somehow, their intelligence network predicted that this will happen before the end of 1944 or early 1945. If they only knew how close their estimates had been!

General Yamashita concentrated his heavy defense in Luzon and installed only pockets of defensive units in Tacloban and Ormoc in Leyte and some parts of Northern Mindanao for a number of reasons. For one thing, they valued more the defense of Luzon rather than the Visayas. Landing in the Visayas or Mindanao would be a lot harder for the Americans because of their thick jungles and forests. Also, the unpredictable and difficult weather patterns in Eastern Visayas would pose a problem for the invading forces. Leyte and Samar islands lie in a corridor that had been called the "typhoon belt" of the archipelago. "Not in these islands," Gen. Yamashita thought.

The Japanese by this time had been thinly spread from the Malayan peninsula,

Singapore, Brunei and in Manila, Philippines. Since General Yamashita's headquarter was in Manila, his crack and highly trained troops that were veterans of Manchuria and Malaya were therefore with him. Because of this, the Japanese Imperial Army had to conscript or hire Korean mercenaries to beef up their thinning forces. A lot of these Korean conscripts ended in the Philippines.

One would be able to tell if the troops were Korean mercenaries or regular Japanese soldiers by the way they conducted themselves with the local population, especially the prisoners. The Korean mercenaries were very cruel, rough and vicious. Filipinos hated them and called them "animals" because of their cruelty.

Captain Hideki Yamaguchi, An Officer and a Gentleman

Most of the regular Japanese soldiers, especially the officers were kinder, more professional and definitely better behaved than their Korean mercenaries. Some, like Captain Hideki Yamaguchi were gentlemen and highly educated. He graduated from the

Imperial Military Academy in Tokyo Japan, the equivalent of the West Point Military Academy in New York, USA. Like the graduates of West Point, Yamaguchi was trained not only to become a loyal soldier for the Emperor, ready to lay down his life for Japan, but also to become a leader and a gentleman. Horror stories of babies being tossed up in the air to be pierced by bayonets and prisoners being decapitated were allegedly done mostly by these Korean mercenaries in the Japanese armed forces.

Captain Yamaguchi owed his good qualities to his distinguished family lineage. His ancestors were genuine Samurais who were guided strictly by the "Bushido", the code of conduct of samurais. He came from a well-to-do and a respected family in Japan. His ancestral family fortune was already flourishing even before the war and his great-grand father was a very successful merchant and trader at Yokohama City. Among the products they traded was hemp from Manila. These were abaca fibers that were used in making ropes. They imported the abaca fibers from Cebu and Mindanao that were produced by Japanese nationals before the war broke out. Yokohama is now the second largest city of Japan (next to Tokyo) in terms of population. It is the capital of Nakagawa Prefecture located south of Tokyo, by Tokyo Bay of the main island of Honshu. The Yamaguchi family owned an eight-story building where they lived and also conducted their business. On the ground floor of the building, and at the center of the spacious lobby made of black marble, is a rectangular glass box mounted on marble pillars. Inside is a samurai sword sheathed in its black scabbard made from buffalo horns. It has the Japanese inscriptions of its Samurai owner, the great-great grandfather of Captain Yamaguchi. This is one of the Yamaguchi clan's prized possessions.

Military Intelligence on Dulag

Based on intelligence gathered by the guerilla units under Colonel Ruperto Kanleon from the Southern part of Leyte, during the summer of 1943, Dulag was identified as a special military target because a large Japanese Garrison had been in existence and thriving in the town since 1942. But unlike most places in the Philippines where Filipinos hated the Japanese garrisons and were hostile to the Japanese occupiers, the people of Dulag seem to have a different story.

The people of Dulag developed a very good relationship with the Japanese occupiers of the town by June of 1943. This was mostly credited to the work of the young and popular Japanese Captain fondly called Captain Yamaguchi by the locals. Captain Yamaguchi, in his early thirties exuded confidence, kindness and fairness that quickly won the trust and admiration of the local population. He arrived at the Garrison about May of 1943 and immediately changed the usual if not familiar harsh and tyrannical policies of his predecessor. He rewrote and promulgated new sets of rules based on mutual trust and respect for the people of Dulag. The same harsh punishments were still in place but only for those found deliberately violating it. If ever punishments had to be given, they were administered with justice and fairness. He employed local people to work in the garrison and paid them as well. He showed concern for the people and was generously paid back by the people of Dulag.

One of these paid workers was Dalisay Borja who brought the Captain food and refreshments daily. For this, Dalisay, her father and mother were given almost unrestricted access to the garrison. Dalisay even had exclusive access inside the Captain's quarters. Dalisay's father naturally became a rich source of information about the Japanese garrison for the Kangleon guerillas operating in Leyte.

However, this tormented Dalisay to no end because of her fear of being discovered and the shame she feels for betraying the trust of their benefactor, Captain Yamaguchi. As a matter of fact, Dalisay was torn between her love for her family and country and the feelings she has developed for Captain Yamaguchi. She was obviously infatuated, being only sixteen. Standing at five feet and three inches, Dalisay had a long wavy hair that fell down to her waist, a smooth silky brown skin and a tantalizing pair of big brown eyes. She was soft spoken, but not annoyingly high-pitched like the Japanese women's voice tone. Her feminine and pleasant voice greatly enhanced her gentle disposition. Her beautiful and ready smile can easily disarm and turn anyone's anger into quiet approval and submission.

Captain Yamaguchi was simply no match to her charm. The relationship that grew between Captain Yamaguchi and Dalisay was of course a highly guarded secret for fear of unfavorable consequences for both. It was not good for any Japanese officer to develop an intimate relationship with any native for security reasons. Unless it is just for mere consorting, an intimate relationship with a native is prohibited for a Japanese officer. For Dalisay, it was also not acceptable for a Waray-wary to consort with the enemy, and any Japanese for that matter. Although the age gap was big, it was not unusual for Filipino females thirteen or fourteen-year-old to be betrothed for marriage during those days. Even so, their relationship was therefore highly prohibited. It was worse than taboo. But young Dalisay likewise easily fell for the kind and winning ways of the Japanese officer and gentleman. They had to communicate very discreetly and act without malice. Their language of affection therefore was expressed in subtle gestures, nods and hidden glances. Both had to cover and control their great desire for intimacy with politeness and formal courtesies. They were afforded some privacy only when Dalisay brought to the Captain's table his favorite food of freshly barbequed fish and white cheese from carabao milk wrapped in banana leaves, prepared by Mana Teresa. Occasionally, Mano Berto would bring to the Captain himself fresh "kinilaw" from his daily catch. Kinilaw is a Visayan version of a raw fish dish steeped in coconut vinegar, green pepper, garlic, red onion and ginger. It is a delicacy among waray-warays but more so for the "sashimi"-eating Japanese Captain. Fresh fish abound in Dulag and most of Leyte. These were the simple pleasures that Captain Yamaguchi enjoyed in his new garrison. The captain would return Dalisay's kindness with trust and fairness in dealing with the locals.

One day, Mang Opoc, a friend of her father came to their house to inform him that he was asked by Captain Yamaguchi to do some carpentry work at the captain's quarters. The two conferred privately making sure that Dalisay did not hear what they were discussing. They were discussing a top-secret matter, involving the guerillas and intelligence reports coming in from couriers up and down Eastern Visayas.

Dalisay always made sure that the Captain knows how much her townmates appreciate his kind gestures in order that his trust and confidence on the people are not lost. This relationship was of mutual benefit for the Japanese military and the people of Dulag.

"I am doing this to your people because of you" exclaims the Captain, whereupon the blushing lass retreats in embarrassment for the flattery.

For these kind gestures she gave the Captain loyalty and genuine caring. She was truly devoted to his physical well-being and safety. It worked both ways. The guerillas will get valuable information about the plans of General Yamashita, the Supreme Commander of the Japanese forces in the Philippines through Mang Berto, while the Captain will be warned of imminent dangers to his life, through Dalisay. This seemed to be a convenient arrangement that did not hurt anyone, at least for a while and at the moment.

But things were about to change.

Treachery or Patriotism or Love?

At the beginning of the summer of 1944, Dalisay learned of an impending attack by the guerillas to the Dulag garrison thru the intelligence gathered by the Japanese.

It was Monday and as usual Dalisay came to the garrison, just before noon carrying her basket filled with steamed rice, kinilaw, barol and boiled camote tops. In a separate but smaller basket are freshly peeled pineapple and red watermelons.

Dalisay set the table like she always did and laid the food spread on the table set for just one person. She did not notice that by the door towards the Commander's private office, Captain Yamaguchi was quietly watching Dalisay do her routine work.

"Please set the table for two today" he politely admonished from behind. Dalisay was slightly startled.

“Oh, for two? Sure, yes sir”, she politely replied. Recovering quickly, she did so as instructed.

“Dalisay san, may I ask you to stay by the kitchen and wait for me to call you in after my guest for lunch has left,” he continued.

This was a little bit odd because first of all the Captain usually eats by himself. He also usually let her leave right away. She was usually asked to come back later to put the plates and the left overs away. But Dalisay thought nothing of it at first.

Shortly after, Dalisay waited at the kitchen which was in the next room and some distance away from where the Captain and his guest would be sitting. She could see the two sitting on the table but she could not hear their conversation.

When the guest arrived Dalisay could tell that the visitor was an officer. It was Major Inoue. Captain Yamaguchi bowed his head lower than his guest’s bow and the guest sat himself on the “cabecera” of the table. After some pleasantries, they promptly ate their lunch while talking in Nihongo between bites but in a low voice.

Shortly after tea, the Japanese Major stood up and both bowed to each other. Dalisay also rose from her chair in the kitchen and waited for the Captain to call her in.

"Dalisay San," the captain finally called her with a wave of his right hand.

"Please listen carefully but you must keep this to yourself and only with the concerned people," the Captain said to her in a very serious tone and stern face.

The Captain carefully explained to Dalisay that their higher command in Manila relayed to them the information of an impending attack by the Americans by the end of the year (1944) or early next year. Not only that. They were warned of a possible attack by the guerillas on the Dulag garrison even before the landings. The garrison was well secured by high walls with barbed wire on top and on the ground footings of the walls. They have towers at every corner of the camp with 30 caliber machine guns mounted in each tower. In addition, Major Inoue confirmed that their request for reinforcements from Luzon and Borneo to defend Leyte and Mindanao in case of an

American invasion late in 1944 or early 1945 were positively endorsed by General Yamashita himself. With these in mind, Captain Yamaguchi was confident that it will be almost impossible or an exercise in futility to attack the garrison by the less equipped Leyte guerillas.

"There is no way they could succeed to overrun this camp," Captain Yamaguchi empathically said to the Dalisay without explaining why.

"There will be a big loss of lives for these guerillas" he continued, "if ever they continue with their foolish plan!"

Captain Yamaguchi looked Dalisay in the eye and said "We can avoid the loss of lives and destruction of this town if you help me."

"Sir, you know I will do anything for our people," she paused, "...and you Sir".

"Then listen to me Dalisay San. Do this for your country and your people, not me," the Captain retorted.

"So, what do we do Sir?" Dalisay replied anxiously trying to control her emotions.

Captain Yamaguchi explained to Dalisay why it was foolish to attack the Dulag garrison, without giving away strategic and important military information. The Captain had been well trained in handling intelligence information and was also very adept in getting his own, from the unknowing but willing Dulag town people. He emphasized to Dalisay that the camp was well defended and heavily armed. The Captain, in half-whisper to Dalisay to dramatize or make it sound like it was certain, said that crack Japanese troops who were veterans from the Malayan campaign were in fact on their way to Leyte via Ormoc. This last one of course was a lie or at best a speculation. What was true was that reinforcements could easily come from Ormoc where there was an airfield and the ports were deep enough for military ship transports, if there were any reinforcements coming. On the other-hand Captain Yamaguchi said that they easily outnumber and can outgun the guerillas in Leyte. This was true. The guerillas were not so many and their weapons were inferior.

"Trust me. Stop them because it is suicide!" he curtly told Dalisay and nearly raising the pitch of his voice. Dalisay obviously did not know anything about the guerillas, how strong or weak they were.

But Dalisay trusted Captain Yamaguchi and believed with all her heart that she would be doing her town, her townspeople and even her brother Luis a favor by listening to and following Captain Yamaguchi's plan.

Overwhelmed by her respect and love for Captain Yamaguchi, and fear for the safety of her countrymen, she went home and explained everything to her father Mano Berto. Mano Berto likewise confirmed the guerillas plan as told him by Mang Opoc, who turned out to be a spy or an asset of Colonel Kangleon's guerillas.

The following day, Dalisay confirmed the plan of the guerillas to Captain Yamaguchi and warned him of what she was told of the guerilla's plan. Her intent was not one of betrayal of the guerillas but one to protect the life of Captain Yamaguchi and avoid unnecessary losses of lives from both sides. With both Captain Yamaguchi and the guerillas being aware of each other's plan, Captain Yamaguchi asked Dalisay to arrange for a secret meeting with the leader of the guerillas to convince the guerillas not to push through and call off the attack. If ever there has to be a firefight, Captain Yamaguchi wants it staged and outside the town of Dulag to avoid collateral damages. This was to avoid the unnecessary loss of lives and let the guerillas save face from their American handlers. Dalisay's father played a role in arranging the meeting. Unknown to Dalisay, the guerillas hatched a treacherous plan to assassinate Captain Yamaguchi. They were using Dalisay to convince Captain Yamaguchi to personally meet them in a meeting. But the Captain did not need any convincing. He wanted the meeting too, but for a different reason.

The Japanese captain was convinced that their superior forces would easily defeat the guerillas and cause death and destruction among the guerillas and the population of Dulag, if the attack happens in Dulag. He wanted to save their military resources for the possible invasion of Leyte by the Americans. Full of trust for both the guerillas and Captain Yamaguchi, Dalisay willingly arranged `for the Captain to meet with the guerillas outside of Dulag through her father. She believed that she was doing her townmates and her beloved Captain Yamaguchi a great favor. This was to save lives.

The road from the valley of Leyte from Carigara to Ormoc was known as the Pinamopoan - Ormoc road. From Limon the road winds its way up through the hills and several ridges along Capoocan, before it gently rolls down to Kanangga and Ormoc. From the point of view of military operators, the short segment of the road from Limon through Kanangga is the most treacherous and perfect for ambush. The road winds through the sides of hills and ridges bisect the road at different points.

On the way to the appointed meeting place, somewhere in the hills of Capoocan, on the way to Ormoc, Captain Yamaguchi and a few select Japanese soldiers set out for the meeting at the appointed time and place, fully armed. Two days passed from the day of the meeting but the Captain and his men have not returned to the garrison. Then the sad news came. Mang Opoc broke the news that on the way to the rendezvous place, the Captain and his men were ambushed and nobody among the Japanese detail survived the ambush. The news of Captain Yamaguchi's death quickly circulated in Dulag. Not surprisingly, the whole town immediately went into mourning. Some even cried at the loss of their Japanese friend. According to Mang Opoc and Mang Berto, the Captain's death saved the lives of the guerillas and destruction of the town. But to Dalisay and the other admirers of the Captain, it was a very costly and an unnecessary price to pay.

Dalisay Borja was inconsolable and her feelings swung between extreme feelings of guilt and anger. Guilt for being a tool in his beloved's death and anger for the guerillas who betrayed her trust. In a period of six short months starting from the summer of 1944, Dalisay Borja would lose the loves of her life, his beloved Captain Yamaguchi in the hands of the guerillas and her mother and father from the shells of the 14 inch guns of US 7th Fleet under the command of Admiral Kinkaid, part of the naval support group for the landing forces of General Douglas MacArthur.

Years later, after the war, the town's people of Dulag would erect a permanent tribute to their beloved Captain Yamaguchi in the center of the town just across the Municipal building, a statue of the Captain. The Japanese veterans of the war would make annual visits to Dulag to pay their respect to the Captain and many of his soldiers who died during the liberation of Leyte. The Rotary Club of Yokohama City, Japan from where the family and descendants of Captain Yamaguchi hailed would make several donations to the town of Dulag: a public library and a school building. This was to honor the memories of Captain Yamaguchi and his brave soldiers. This was a rare and continuing tribute to an Officer and a Gentleman, Captain Yamaguchi of the Japanese Imperial Army. But this is getting ahead of our story.

During times of war, the value of life is cheap if not with a price depending one's value to the military. The value of life is relative and a function of the value of military objectives to one's circumstance. Under normal circumstances life is considered so precious that its value is priceless and the same for all. A person's life is just as valuable as anybody's, whether one is a janitor or a politician or a rich landowner. During the Leyte landings, the battery gun-master decides who lives and who dies. The value of life is determined by its strategic value in relation to military objectives. The lives of Mano Berto and Mana Teresa were valued just like that. They were to be part of the collateral damage of the landings. They became mere statistics, the first casualties of Operation KING TWO, the code name for the Liberation of the Philippines.

CHAPTER 5

The Leyte Landings

"People of the Philippines, I have returned! By the grace of Almighty God, our forces stand again on Philippine soil."

As planned by the Joint Chiefs-of-Staff presided over by General Douglas MacArthur, the Supreme Commander of the US Armed Forces in the Far East (USAFFE), the liberation of the Philippine Archipelago was launched in the early morning of October 19, 1944 at Palo, Leyte.

The first of the thousands of shells fired by the destroyers from the Third Fleet of Admiral William Halsey and the Seventh Fleet of Admiral Kinkaid fell on the coastal towns of Tanauan, Tolosa and Dulag. From the bridge of flagship Nashville, MacArthur could see the flashes of red, orange and white as the shells exploded among the thick vegetation that covered the targets. It was very early in the morning and the sun had not risen yet from the eastern horizon. It was very difficult to determine the effect of the bombardment not only because it was a dark and moonless when the bombardment started but also because the coast was covered by coconut trees and thick vegetation. It was monsoon season and the leaves of trees, bushes and grass were at their tallest and thickest. There were fishermen and their families who lived by the shorelines of these towns and it was simply impossible for anyone to have warned all of them to evacuate in time. There were casualties for sure but many were able to evade the direct hits of shells because of the quick thinking and heroics of three brave boy scouts.

Weeks before the bombardment, the guerillas of Colonel Ruperto Kangleon who operated in Southern Leyte received information about the planned Leyte landings by the Americans and tried to spread the news without alerting the Japanese. But the Japanese knew that the Americans would come and yet did not realize that the main landing was already upon them and it was going to be Leyte.

For one thing the monsoon season was the worst time to launch a landing and Leyte happens to lie along the typhoon corridor of the archipelago. The rainfall was usually very heavy during monsoons and Leyte and Samar soils become boggy if not outright muddy. Heavy equipment would sink in deep mud and transport movement therefore becomes very difficult if not impossible. Naturally, the Japanese thought that the very idea of launching the liberation of the Philippines in October was quite absurd. The Japanese strategists in Tokyo therefore predicted that the Americans will most likely attack in

November 1944 at the earliest or February, 1945 at the latest.

But to win a war, one must think differently and must not be predictable. What the Japanese strategists were thinking was too predictable and too logical.

Luis Borja came down from the mountains of Abuyog and Mahaplag, Leyte and reached Dulag after a week of walking and negotiating hidden trails in the jungles of Leyte. He traveled alone, just armed with a bolo slung on his waist. He used this to make his own path through the jungle and brought with him a kilo of rice and some salt to sustain him. He could not carry a firearm to evade his real identity just in case he encountered a Japanese patrol. Possession of a gun or a rifle was an easy give away to the Japanese military. On the other hand, farmers, fishermen and most natives carry a bolo everyday as part of their work attire.

Luis reached Dulag in the evening of October 18. The day before, he already heard of sporadic bombardments coming from the direction of Leyte Gulf. These came from the gunships and B-17 bombers of the US Third and Seventh Fleet, testing for Japanese resistance and trying to locate Japanese military placements in the landing areas. Catmon Hill in Dulag became an important target.

Hungry, tired and haggard, Luis first sought the help of his and Dalisay's childhood friends, boy scouts Val Abello and Enteng Tastin.

"Val and Enteng, may da ako sumat nga importante sugad imo nga tanan," Luis said in waray. (Val and Enteng, I have a very important message for all of you.)

"Kay ano man?" replied Val after giving Luis a glass of water. (What is it?)

"Lakat nyan tanan, pangiwas kamo nga tanan ligid ha dagat! Waray na tanong!", Luis said in a single breath. (All of you must immediately leave the beaches. And do not ask any more questions.)

"We have to tell everyone to leave now or die!" he said with finality.

That night, the boy scouts went house to house to warn everyone to leave the beaches.

A lot of them did but they had to do it quietly and under the cover of darkness for fear of being discovered by the Japanese soldiers stationed at the camp and at Catmon Hill. Luis meanwhile went to see his sister Dalisay and his parents nearby at the foot of Catmon Hill.

It was Dalisay who woke up holding a "gasera" (a kerosene filled jar with a wick, commonly used by natives as light instead of a candle) and let Luis in their hut.

"Tatay, Nanay, lakat na kita nyan," Luis whispered to his surprised family. (Mom and dad, let us leave now.)

"Han mga Kano nag-abot ka-kulop. Bombahin han tanan dagat, "he whispered to them. (The Americans arrived last night. They will bomb this place and all the beaches.)

Dalisay had other things in her mind. Did Luis see Captain Yamaguchi? How did he die? Was he with the group who assassinated the Japanese Captain?

A couple of weeks before and during the appointed day of rendezvous between the Captain's squad and the guerillas, Luis was in fact with a company of men sent by Colonel Kangleon to meet the Japanese. He confirmed to Dalisay the encounter that ended the Captain's life but will not admit or call it an assassination. They reported it as an encounter. Luis loved his sister and did not want to further hurt her feelings. He knew the fondness and mutual respect that developed between Dalisay and Captain Yamaguchi, and the special treatment his family was getting from the Japanese. He was grateful to this but more importantly, he and Colonel Kangleon encouraged the relationship in order to gather and keep the valuable intelligence information coming so that they could in turn relay it to the Americans.

A relationship like this was forbidden by both the Japanese and Filipinos, especially Mano Berto and Luis. But for the love of country, the relationship was tolerated and was even encouraged. It resulted in the steady flow of quality and reliable intelligence information about the Japanese plans on the defense of Leyte. But Luis knew that for Dalisay this was not just patriotism. Her feelings for the Captain maybe "puppy love" but they were real. Luis himself will be the last person to accept a Japanese and an enemy for a boyfriend of his sister, but for the love of her and for the higher purposes that it served the guerilla movement, he had to tolerate if not approve the relationship. His only concern was not to hurt Dalisay so that they could move on and face the more immediate business of surviving the bombardment and liberation of Leyte.

"Ma-lakat na ako, lakat na kamo liwat" said Luis after a few minutes of lingering. (I have to leave now. You must also leave now.) Every minute counted because the main bombardment to soften the beaches for the landings was about to commence.

The Heroism of the Three former Boy Scouts to save Civilian Lives

On October 18, 1944, two days before the main landing of the massive US and Allied naval forces on the shores of Palo, Tanauan, Tolosa and Dulag, Leyte, three childhood friends of Dalisay and former members of the Boy Scouts of the Philippines came out to an open spot along the beach of what is now Barangay Telegrafo, Municipality of Tolosa,

Leyte to warn and stop the US warships against bombarding the shores of Tolosa and Dulag.

Scout Valeriano I. Abello fashioned two white semaphore flags out of cotton diaper linens and began sending this message to ship No. 467 anchored off the Tolosa Beach:

"Don't Bomb the beaches. There are civilians. If possible, let me direct the shelling."

With these three short sentences, Scout Abello, with the help of Scouts Antero Justin, Sr., and Scout Vicente Tiston saved thousands of lives in Tolosa that fateful day when the pre-landing bombardment of the beaches of Palo, Tanauan, Dulag and Tolosa started. Thanks to the earlier warning by Luis Borja.

Later that night, they paddled their way into ship No. 467 and helped direct the bombardment of the beaches in Dulag and Tolosa, away from the main populace.

The nipa hut of Mano Berto and Mana Teresa was right at the foot of Catmon Hill where there was a Japanese gun placement and a military installation. Dalisay wanted to desperately warn her parents to leave the place as soon as Luis left. But Mano Berto hesitated because he wanted to save his fishing nets and his boat. It was too late. The bombardment had begun. Between flurries of colorful explosions of red, orange, white and black smoke, the nipa hut was blown away into small pieces of wood. Dalisay who was bloodied and hurt by a shrapnel that tore into her left leg, pulled herself away from what was left of the hut and saw the bloodied bodies of her mother and father sprawled by the beach, still holding on to a fishing net.

Fortunately, a guerilla unit who were helping direct the line of fire saw the bleeding Dalisay. They immediately tied a tourniquet around her leg, wrapped her wound with bandage and pulled her away to safety. Dalisay lost consciousness and found herself among the casualties of the bombardment at the Palo Infirmary when she regained consciousness. The infirmary was once the Palo Cathedral of the Catholic church that was converted into a hospital weeks before the Leyte landings.

After being warned by three young scouts, using improvised semaphore flags out of rags not to bomb the beaches of Tolosa and directing their fire in selected targets in Dulag, heavy bombardment commenced before the crack of dawn on October 19, 1944. Tons of shells fired in cadence and quick succession from almost a hundred warships of the Third and Seventh Fleets rained on the eastern shores of Leyte.

The following morning, October 20, 1944, from the deck of USS Nashville, the command ship of General Douglas MacArthur for the Leyte Landings, the General surveyed the still smoking shores of Red Beach using his binoculars, as hundreds of landing crafts bearing troops, armored vehicles, ammunitions and artillery pieces quickly made beachheads and secured the landing areas. By noon of the Leyte landing, almost a hundred thousand troops have made it to the beaches of Tolosa, Dulag and Palo, Leyte. Tons of equipment, supplies and other war materials were also safely on the beaches of Leyte.

Also, on the deck all geared up for the landing were Resident Commissioner in the US, Gen. Carlos P. Romulo, Philippine Commonwealth President Sergio Osmena, a couple of close military aides of the general and of course Macario Depuesto.

Before noon time, the beachmaster gave General MacArthur the go-signal to land and board the launch that will bring him to shore with his immediate landing party. But to the General's chagrin, he was informed that his landing party will have to wade on knee-high water because the shores were too shallow and the transports could not come closer to the beach. The image of the moment when General MacArthur waded in the waters of Palo beach along with President Sergio Osmena, General Carlos P. Romulo, two of his close-in military aides and his medical aide Macario Depuesto, was forever frozen in time by a historic black and white photo taken by an American military correspondent. The moment was also immortalized by the Palo Leyte Landing Shrine built by the Philippine Department of Tourism during the Marcos regime, in the 1970s.

Upon reaching the beach, and using a megaphone and speakers specifically set up for the dramatic occasion, General Douglas MacArthur uttered his famous words:

"People of the Philippines, I have returned! By the grace of Almighty God, our forces stand again on Philippine soil."

As expected, the event was front-page and headline material with the New York Times. If there was CNN then, they would have broadcast the whole event live!

This was an excerpt from the New York Times' story featuring the message of President Franklin Delano Roosevelt to the Filipino people on October 21, 1944:

"On this occasion of the return of General MacArthur to Philippine soil with our airmen, our soldiers and our sailors, we renew our pledge. We and our Philippine brothers in arms – with the help of Almighty God – will drive out the invader; we will destroy his power to wage war again, and we will restore a world of dignity and freedom- a world of confidence and honesty and peace."

Dalisay and her parents Mano Berto and Mana Teresa, in spite of the earlier warnings by Luis, were caught during the first round of bombardments just before 6 am of October 19. Mano Berto and Mana Teresa were dead on the spot while Dalisay was hit on the left leg by a shrapnel of the exploding shell that killed her parents.

At about this time, Dalisay had been transferred to Palo and was taken by her boy scout friends to the infirmary in view of her wound that was in danger of getting infected. The Palo Cathedral was quickly filled by injured civilians like Dalisay Borja. His parents were quickly buried at the Dulag Catholic cemetery, without the benefit of the usual Roman Catholic burial rites.

By 1 pm, the landing forces of the US Sixth Army have pushed inland by almost four kilometers. In Dulag, the garrison was already abandoned by the Japanese forces days before. They retreated towards Dagami, Capoocan and Ormoc. Also, days earlier, General Yamashita ordered Major Inoue to "hold the line at all cost" at the ridges of Capoocan, Leyte. Catmon Hill which was called Hill 120 by the American forces was once again flying the American flag. In Tacloban, the old Montejo Mansion was once again converted to the headquarters of Gen. MacArthur while the Price Mansion was being prepared for President Osmena and his cabinet members.

The successful landing by the Sixth Army of the US liberating forces was now poised to move inland towards Ormoc and Samar.

Still the Japanese General did not believe!

Lt. General Sosaku Suzuki, the commanding general of the Japanese Thirty-fifth Army that was based in Cebu realized that the Americans were landing in Leyte only on the 19th of October, 1944. It was too late to do anything to defend the eastern shorelines of Leyte. He informed General Yamashita of the landings and even sent him a copy of MacArthur's black and white photos of the Leyte landing that was flashed all over the world.

"I do not believe this. Do not be deceived. This was a mock-up of the landings in New Guinea!" said General Yamashita.

Years later after the war, Yamashita admitted that this was something he truly regretted. Had he known that such an important military leader would himself be at the war front, wading in the shallow waters of

Leyte, “he would have sent to Leyte all the armed forces and suicide bombers under his command, just to avenge the death Admiral Yamamoto”. Yamamoto was the Japanese Admiral who led the attack in Pearl Harbor on December 8, 1941. He was killed when his flight from New Guinea was intercepted by American fighter planes.

CHAPTER 6

The Battle of the Leyte Gulf, October 23 to 26, 1944

"But the favorable outcome of this great sea battle in favor of the US and its allies almost never happened."

As the landings progressed bringing in a steady flow of personnel and war materials into Leyte, the battle of the Leyte Gulf raged.

The greatest naval battle of all time based on gross tonnage of ships involved, number of airplanes, armed personnel, size and area of battleship-to-battleship engagements and the impact of its results to the course of history was undoubtedly the Battle of Leyte Gulf that began in the early morning of October 23, 1944.

Here is why many agree that Battle of Leyte Gulf in 1944 was the greatest ever:

Impact on History and Final Outcome of the Second World War

The outcome of the naval battle that started on the early morning hours of October 23, 1944 off the Gulf of Leyte, Philippines resulted in the final destruction of the mighty Imperial Japanese Navy (IJN). The Battle of Leyte Gulf raged from October 23 through 26, 1944. It was the largest naval battle ever fought - ending the reign of the Imperial Japanese Navy (IJN) in the Pacific and its last sortie as a naval force to contend with. Leyte Gulf also was the scene of the first organized use of Kamikaze (suicide) bombers by the Japanese. *But the favorable outcome of this great sea battle in favor of the US and its allies almost never happened.*

Maybe it was again a case of sheer luck or “kismet” (fate) that the Japanese Central Force, under the command of Vice Admiral Kurita suddenly disengaged after successfully breaking through the San Bernardino Strait instead of bombarding the largely unprotected Leyte Landings. To this day there had been no clear explanation that was offered by both the US Navy and the Japanese Imperial Navy regarding this unexpected move by Vice Admiral Kurita.

As agreed by the Joint Chiefs-of-Staff of the US Armed forces, General Douglas MacArthur was to implement *King Two* to launch the liberation of the Philippine archipelago from the Japanese. The US Sixth Army would be involved on the ground in this liberation campaign. At the ensuing Battle of the Leyte Gulf, the US Third Fleet under the command of Admiral William Halsey, and the US Seventh Fleet under the command of Admiral Thomas Kinkaid would provide cover for the landings. If need be, they would engage the Imperial Japanese Navy, consisting of the Northern Force, under the command of

Isaburo Ozawa, the Center Force, Commanded by Vice Admiral Takeo Kurita and the Southern Force, Commanded by Vice Admirals Shoji Nishimura and Kyode Shima. As it turned out, neither of the contending forces had accurate information about each other's strength before the actual engagement.

SHO-GO 1 – A Pincer Attack of the Leyte Landings

The Japanese Imperial Navy implemented Shō-Gō 1 which called for the attack of the American forces at the Leyte landings. It was a bold and ingenious plan that almost worked. The plan was triggered by the chance encounter by the Japanese air patrols with the American reconnaissance planes during the exploratory bombing of targets in Luzon, Leyte and Mindanao by the Americans sometime in July, 1944. *Shō-Gō* 1 called for Vice Admiral Jisaburō Ozawa's ships known as the "Northern Force" to lure the main American naval forces, the US Third Fleet under the Command of Admiral William F. Halsey, Jr. away from Leyte Gulf. The

Northern Force, the decoy, would have several aircraft carriers in the plan. But these carriers would have very few aircraft and trained aircrew. The carriers would serve as the main bait. As the U.S. Third Fleet were lured away, two other surface forces would advance on Leyte from the west. The "Southern Force" under Vice Admirals Shoji Nishimura and Kiyohide Shima would strike at the landing area via the Surigao Strait. The "Center Force" under Vice Admiral Takeo Kurita, by far the most powerful of the attacking forces—would pass through the Philippine Sea and proceed to the San Bernardino Strait, turn southwards, and then join the Southern Force in pounding the Leyte landing area.

The strategy was simple but sound. Vice Admiral Ozawa's Northern Force, composed of light carriers with hardly any airplane on it would lure away the mighty Third Fleet of Admiral Halsey, which really comprised the brunt of the US naval forces who was supposed to guard the Leyte Landings. The Center Force commanded by Admiral Kurita, was in fact the only remaining but still deadly main naval force of the Imperial Japanese

Navy. This fleet included their super-battleships Yamato and Musashi. In the plan, they would be joined by the Southern Force, commanded Vice Admirals Nishimura and Shima, to attack the American forces and the Leyte landings. The Center Force will sail into San Bernardino Strait before it makes a right turn and sail south towards Leyte Gulf, while the Southern Force will enter the Leyte Gulf through the Surigao Strait, turn north towards the Leyte Gulf.

As it actually turned out, Admiral William Halsey took the bait and his fleet, which was supposed to guard and cover the American landings in Leyte left the eight-kilometer-long beaches unguarded.

The Japanese command, just like the Americans, suffered the same problem of lack of unity of command in their implementation of Shogo-1. Admirals Ozawa, Kurita, Nishimura and Shima reported to Admiral Toyoda, the Supreme Commander of the IJN who held court at their headquarters in Tokyo. The occupying Imperial Japanese Army and airmen on the other hand was commanded by General Tomoyuki Yamashita, who was based in Manila. There was an utter lack of coordination and communication between these two major Commands of the Japanese armed forces. Valuable information gathered by the Japanese reconnaissance in their previous encounters with the advance bombers of Halsey did not reach the Navy command in Tokyo in time. At this waning period of the Pacific war, the Tokyo command was mainly pre-occupied with the defense of Japan while Yamashita seemed to have been left on his own to defend the Japanese occupied areas in the Philippines, particularly Luzon.

The Americans on the other hand had their own problems on their side of the opposing forces. Their organization was in fact more complicated than the Japanese. The Americans also had to deal with strong personalities of their commanders. Admiral Nimitz had the more direct command and authority over the Third Fleet of William Halsey from his headquarters in Pearl Harbor. The landing Forces including the Seventh Fleet of Admiral Kinkaid and the Sixth Army were under the Command of General Douglas MacArthur. Each main command can direct their forces independently of each other. Their coordination was set by their commanders at the top level (Nimitz and MacArthur as far as the Leyte landings were concerned) and orders have to go all the way up, before it goes down to the commanders in the field for implementation. The American chain of command for the liberation of the Pacific took a longer route than the Japanese.

By some stroke of luck, precise timing and execution by the US Seventh Fleet, the "Southern Force" under Shoji Nishimura and Kiyohide Shima was stopped and nearly annihilated at the Battle of Sibuyan Sea, in the hands of Admiral Kinkaid's Seventh Fleet. This battle was described by military naval analysts as like their textbook description of an ideal naval battle where the Americans would be able to "cross the T" of the opposing naval forces. Admirals Kinkaid and Oldendorf laid out a plan to ambush the Japanese Southern Force at the Sibuyan Channel. The Sibuyan Channel was a narrow and treacherous channel where there was limited area for maneuvering by large vessels such as the Japanese naval warships. Nishimura and Shima's fleet encountered losses as early as its Sulu Sea passage. The American Seventh fleet, compared to the Japanese fleet were mostly composed of light carriers, and thinly armored destroyers. But the ferocious sniping by the American PT boats and submarines effectively intimidated the Japanese fleet that before they could reach the Leyte Gulf, major losses were inflicted on the Japanese fleet. Technology also aided the American forces as many ships in their fleet were equipped with radar guided guns. Their guns were more accurate than the Japanese guns, scoring more hits than the Japanese could. Nishimura and Shima were forced to disengage and make a U-turn from the Surigao Strait, back to the Sibuyan channel, instead of proceeding to Samar and Leyte where the landings lay like sitting-ducks. The surviving ships had to limp their way back to their base in Borneo. It was hard to believe that the sniping of small PT boats and much smaller American warships stopped the Japanese fleet that was heavier in tonnage but lesser in number. The ferocity with which the tiny American warships stood their ground led the Japanese to believe that this was part of the big and powerful US Third Fleet who were waiting for them in ambush.

Similarly the "Center Force" under Vice Admiral Takeo Kurita whose fleet included the battle ship “Musashi”, twin of the mighty battle ship “Yamato”, received early harassment from US submarines when they entered the South China Sea (now called West Philippine Sea) off the island of Palawan. Admiral Kurita himself had to be rescued from his flagship Atago after it was hit by torpedoes from the American submarines Darter and Dace. Kurita had to transfer to the Yamato and made it his flagship while the damaged Atago managed to stay afloat to be towed back to their base in Singapore.

In the meantime, Admiral Halsey, as authorized by Nimitz to “execute as necessary” while performing as the main cover to protect the Leyte landings, was convinced that he was pursuing the main Japanese Naval fleet and would not let go of the opportunity to destroy it this time. Earlier at the Battle of Philippine Sea, Halsey missed a similar opportunity by not searching hard enough to locate and pursue the enemy. He felt that he was doing the more strategic and important mission of destroying the Japanese main fleet rather than just to guard the Leyte landings. Well, he thought that this was the main Japanese fleet he was pursuing. Besides, he felt that Admiral Kinkaid's Seventh Fleet was capable and sufficient enough to do the job of guarding the landings. He did not know that the main Japanese naval force, the Central Force commanded by Kurita was in fact coming in via San Bernardino Strait to destroy the Leyte landing forces. For lack of timely information, bogged down by radio silence and outright miscommunication, he proceeded to run after an insignificant if not a strategically useless Japanese fleet that was just intended as a decoy, Ozawa's Northern Force. They were expendable as far as the Japanese command was concerned. He also did not know that the Seventh fleet was severely undermanned and outgunned by Kurita's fleet if the Japanese main force managed to reach the Leyte Gulf. Worse, the fleet was running low on ammunitions after the fierce battle of Sibuyan Sea and Surigao Strait. Admiral Kinkaid desperately sent messages to Nimitz for support and reinforcement from the Third Fleet which had the firepower and battleships to stop Kurita's Center Force from entering the Leyte Gulf. But Halsey was now too far north in pursuit of Ozawa and would not reach the Leyte Gulf in time to stop Kurita even if he got the first of the urgent messages.

But for some reasons that up to now could not be explained, Kurita disengaged and turned north leaving the battle that ensued upon its successful passage through the San Bernardino Strait. Earlier, they engaged the light remnants of the Seventh Fleet but was beset by lack of coordination of attack. They too were hampered by their strict radio silence. They could not use the vastly superior 18-inch guns of the Yamato to full use while their smaller battleships did not have the accuracy of the radar guided but smaller guns of the Seventh Fleet. The 14-inch and 16-inch guns from the American battleships scored hits and did damage on the smaller destroyers of Kurita. But their shells simply bounced off the heavy armor of the Yamato. For the first time in battle, the Japanese employed the use of the "Kamikaze" or the "divine wind" suicide bombers. These were Japanese Zero planes whose pilots specially trained in their bases at Clark airbase in Pampanga to attack and crash their airplanes on the American warships.

Call it luck but the Japanese thought that a big ambush was awaiting them and did not believe that the Americans would leave the hapless landings at the coast line of Leyte unprotected. They instead wanted to save their remaining naval forces for the defense of Japan. But the Japanese could have destroyed the American forces that landed in Leyte, if Kurita proceeded. *Had they succeeded in this, the liberation of the Philippines would have been doubtful or at best, at risk, according to Morison (Leyte, Boston, 1963).* For lack of timely communication between the Tokyo Headquarters and the fleets of Kurita, Nishimura and Shima, and also among the three Japanese fleets owing to their own strict radio silence, lack of coordination and effective communication, the Japanese attack disintegrated to confusion.

According to Commodore Morrison (USN Ret), declassified accounts of what happened confirmed that Admiral Halsey took the bait, hook, line and sinker from Vice Admiral Jisaburō Ozawa's Northern Force and left the Leyte landings open for attack. Unknown to the Japanese, Halsey was too far up north in pursuit of Ozawa, to be able to return and cover the landings in time. Had the Japanese Center and Southern forces continued to Samar and Leyte to attack the landings, they would have disposed of the lighter opposition. The US Seventh Fleet, the only fleet left to guard the landings had severely inferior ships and were running out of ammunitions. But the Japanese did not know these. Both the Center and Southern forces' strict radio silence took its toll on the Japanese. These actually saved the day for the Americans. The remaining land-based airplanes of Yamashita could have also helped but due to lack of direct and effective communications with the Tokyo command, the Japanese were not able to use their tactical advantages to help their cause. Both of the opposing forces suffered from poor communications and lack of unity of command. But the ensuing confusion favored the Americans more than the Imperial Japanese Navy. The gods and even the "divine wind" were on the side of the Americans.

Extent and Geographic Size of Battle

The battle of Leyte Gulf involved thousands of square miles of the Pacific

Ocean, from as far down as the Surigao Straight and Sulu Seas on the south, Guam on the East and the Formosa islands on the North where Admiral Halsey was in hot pursuit of the JIN Northern Force. The battle consisted of three major engagements: The Battle of Surigao Strait, The Battle of Sibuyan Sea and the Battle Off Cape Engano, north of the Batanes island group, near Formosa.

Units and Strength of the Naval Forces Involved

The battle involved about 370 ships from both sides (Japan/Australia 300 versus Japan 67+) and more than 1,800 planes (US 1500, Japan 300+). It took the US Navy several months to officially report what happened at the Battle of the Leyte Gulf because the battle "had been too large, involved too many U.S. military personnel, and had resulted in too much loss of life just to ignore". It involved the last of the only two "battleship-to-battleship" shooting engagements during World War II (the first one involving the battle at Guadalcanal).

This was the summarized tabulation of the losses and casualties from both sides at the

Battle of Leyte Gulf according to Commodore Morison:

US Casualties – 3,000	Japanese Casualties – 12,500
US Losses:	Japanese Losses:
1 Light Carriers	1 Fleet Carrier
2 Escort Carriers	3 Light Carriers
2 Destroyers	3 Battleships
1 Destroyer Escort sunk	10 Cruisers
200+ planes	11 Destroyers Sunk
	300 planes

By October 26, 1944, the news of the withdrawal of the last battleship of the once mighty Japanese Imperial Navy, the Center Force under Vice Admiral Kurita from engagement with the American naval forces protecting the landings was jubilantly received by both Admiral Nimitz in Hawaii and the headquarters of General Douglas MacArthur in Leyte.

The great battle of Leyte Gulf came to an end and the Leyte landings were saved and secured.

CHAPTER 7

Love at First Sight at the Infirmary

"Nobody knew that this was actually the beginning of a beautiful romance."

General MacArthur on the third day after landing decided to inspect the Palo Cathedral infirmary where he was told that civilian casualties were confined. Palo, like most rural communities in the Philippines before the war, did not have the primary health care facilities that one can easily find in small towns and cities today. In fact, many Filipinos live and die without even seeing a university-trained doctor in their lifetime. They depend on "Tambals" or quack doctors or "Herbularios" or herb doctors for their primary medical care. It is interesting to note that in the Philippines, one of the most successful programs of the so-called "Barefoot Doctors" took root in Palo, Leyte after the war. The University of the Philippines of the Visayas instituted their special medical program for "Barefoot Doctors" in Palo, Leyte, right next to the infirmary (Palo Cathedral) and the headquarters of Gen. Douglas MacArthur. Every year, they turn out doctors who serve in the barrios from their graduates.

Among those confined in the infirmary was Dalisay Borja who could not walk as her inflamed left leg was too painful to move about. General MacArthur was conferring with the medical staff when he was told that some of those confined would need surgery that cannot be done at the Palo Infirmary. He instructed his Medical Aide-De-Camp,

Macario Depuesto to take a look at the situation and cause the transfer of those needing immediate surgery to their military hospital nearby. One of these patients was Dalisay Borja. She needed immediate surgery to save her leg from amputation because a shrapnel was still imbedded in the leg wound that was caused by the American bombing of the beaches prior to the landings.

Macario immediately caught the sight of Dalisay who was still writhing in pain. Her once clear and big brown eyes were now red, teary and reduced to a squint. Not wasting any time, Macario personally directed and assisted her transfer to their nearest military medical care unit where they have trained surgeons, anti-biotics and all the medical supplies they would need for the surgery. Dalisay was wheeled in the make-shift surgery tent and the nurses quickly prepared her for surgery.

Thank God, the operation took less than an hour primarily because no amputation was necessary. Dalisay slept like a baby through it all. The attending surgeon removed the shrapnel from her left leg. It was almost one and a half inches long and half an inch wide. Powerful anti-biotics along with dextrose were intravenously administered to prevent sepsis and dehydration. Macario for some reason could not leave Dalisay's side from the time Dalisay was sedated for surgery, until she woke up about an hour-and-a-half later. Dalisay could barely see after surgery. She could only figure out blurred outlines of the faces of people around her. She has not even talked to his benefactor, Macario.

While waiting for Dalisay to regain consciousness, Macario was told of Dalisay's ordeal, the loss of her parents and the important role they played in getting intelligence from the enemy. What Macario was not told or did not know was that she was also grieving for the loss of a third loved one, one of their enemies. No one really knew of the secret love affair between Dalisay and the late Captain Yamaguchi. What people were told was that she and her father were responsible for the successful assassination of the Japanese officer a few months before the Leyte landings.

It was therefore a combination of pity and real empathy for Dalisay that Macario felt. He of course first saw Dalisay at her worst physical appearance, sick, haggard and writhing in pain. It was difficult to look pretty or even cheerful under those circumstances. Yet there was an unexplainable attraction and connection that drew Macario to Dalisay, among the hundreds of patients confined at the Palo infirmary.

When she finally became conscious and awake, Macario too was just half awake, almost in stupor for lack of sleep and was startled when she attempted to talk. Macario motioned the nurse for a glass of water or something to give to Dalisay.

> "Kumusta ka na? Ano ang pakiramdam mo?" Macario asked in Tagalog. ("How are you? How are you feeling?"). There was of course no response because Dalisay did not speak Tagalog. Save from a weak smile, she did not really respond. Feeling by now that they were not communicating well, Macario asked her again, this time in English, "How are you feeling?"

All this time, the nurse on duty was observing and could not help but intervene. The nurse could speak English and the local dialect Waray-waray. She immediately sprung into action and translated for Dalisay what Macario was saying in English. Macario asked the nurse to tell Dalisay in waray that he was the one who brought her to surgery and that he was with General Douglas MacArthur, as if to impress her.

"Please tell her that I am also a trained physical therapist and I will make sure that she recovers and walks again," he told the nurse as if asking for his patient's acceptance.

Finally, Dalisay broke into a full smile, after hearing the latter. Once again, her beautiful and expressive eyes came back to life, along with her natural charms.

"Damo nga salamat po." ("Thank you very much sir.") she meekly replied to Macario.

Macario breathed with a sigh of relief after that, thinking that he had finally opened a conversation with this woman whom he seemed to like even before he could know her.

That was all she needed to say that evening to make Macario feel good and excited again. It also had been a long time since he last felt this way. In fact, he could not remember feeling this way at all. The war and his work with General MacArthur's staff did not give him a lot of opportunities to fall in love. It had been all work and no play. That evening, Macario left her with the nurse promising that he will come back to check on her progress the following day. Actually, he could not get Dalisay off his mind even when he got back to his tent at the command center of General MacArthur.

In the next couple of weeks, Dalisay progressively became stronger and healthier as her wound healed. Everyday Macario would visit and chat with her in English and sign language. Once in a while the nurse would be called to translate but they were communicating a lot better.

Macario wanted to explain to Dalisay how the physical therapy works with the help of the nurse who knew how to speak waray. The therapy naturally would involve a lot of touching and Macario was afraid that Dalisay might not take it well. Worse, she might take it with malice. The last thing Macario wanted was for Dalisay to think that he was just taking advantage of her situation. In his mind Macario would love to touch her. How he longed to caress her and maybe kiss her too. These were the hidden feelings that Macario entertained in his private reverie. This was fantasy. Waking up from this daydream, Macario had to figure out a way to explain to Dalisay that the touching was really for medical reasons.

"Please tell her and explain to her that my job as a physical therapist requires that I touch and gently massage her leg muscles. I need to do this so she can walk again without a limp. To do this, we have to see to it that the wound and incisions heal properly without damaging the normal elasticity of her leg muscles," Macario lengthily explained to the nurse, trying to be as technical and as professional as he could.

The nurse translated in Waray but Macario was not sure that she did a good job of explaining. For one thing Macario felt that the translation was too short. She might have missed important words. He thought that the nurse could have done better because after her explanation, Dalisay's eyebrows nearly came together in seeming disapproval.

It was a comical scene to say the least. But of course, Dalisay was just being modest. To a Filipina lass, modesty means no touch. Certainly not by a stranger at the very least. But Macario was very persistent and he finally made a very convincing if not a compelling case. He probably learned this from his boss. He had to do what he had to do as a professional physical therapist. Dalisay eventually acquiesced and cooperated. She did so even reluctantly. The thought of not being able to walk gracefully again was a small price to pay in the name of modesty. The prospect of not being able to walk was far less desirable than this stranger touching her leg. Macario had always done his job as physical therapist very professionally, like it was a second nature to him. He performed the task on the general with efficiency and masterful dexterity. But for some unexplained reasons, he was nervous and very tentative as he started the therapy with Dalisay. He could not hide his clumsiness from his patient. She felt it and wanted to let him know it was okay. But she too was nervous and was also afraid to show her appreciation. But time was always kind to those who wait patiently. In no time, the healer regained his composure and confidence while the patient became more receptive and appreciative of the service.

Both did not know where this situation was leading to. But it was obvious that there was a mutual and positive connection that developed between the two. Nobody knew that this was actually the beginning of a beautiful romance. Macario in the meantime asked for a temporary relief from his physical therapy duties for General MacArthur until Dalisay could walk.

The daily physical therapy that started awkwardly if not comically, became special occasions to learn from each other's lives and to learn how to communicate. Dalisay would teach him some common waray words, while Macario started teaching Dalisay how to converse in English and Tagalog.

By the third week, Dalisay was now able to walk without help but with just a cane and a mild limp. On one hand, Macario was happy of Dalisay's progress, but on the other, he did not want the therapy to end. Sooner or later he will have to have other reasons or excuses to see her.

CHAPTER 8

Coming Back from the Dead

"Feeling betrayed by a loved one was far worse than being used, even for a noble cause."

The Leyte landing by all accounts and standards was a very successful one. KING TWO was launched and off on a great start. There were very few casualties for the landing forces, considering the total number of troops, and the volume and tonnage of materials landed. By day A+5 (October 25) nearly 100,000 troops have poured into Leyte and 20,000 tons of equipment and supplies were likewise on hard ground. In another week, almost 200,000 troops would have landed that will fan out of Tacloban to secure the whole of Leyte and Samar and start the drive north to Luzon.

The slow road to Ormoc

However, the monsoon season was upon Leyte and continuous heavy rains wreaked havoc to the advancing American troops. Tacloban itself was mired with mud and silt as the heavy armored cars, six-by-six trucks and weapons carriers plied daily the main roads of Tacloban. The four-wheeled “MacArthur jeeps” became the transport of choice but even this versatile utility vehicle would be stuck in deep mud or bogs on the dirt roads leading north and northwest to Ormoc Bay.

The main defensive force left by General Yamashita in Leyte was to escape through the Ormoc Bay where transport ships were anchored and the Ormoc airstrip were still held and defended by the Japanese. After abandoning Dulag, General Yamashita drew a line of defense that extended from the steep hills of Carigara and Capoocan to the gently rolling hills towards Ormoc Bay. They called this line of defense in Leyte the "Yamashita Line". The topography of these areas towards Ormoc presented a major problem to the advancing and pursuing American troops.

The Leyte island's geography is such that the middle of the island is lined by sharp mountains from north to south that rolled down to the sea on each side of the island. To reach Ormoc from Tacloban, the troops had to drive through the winding roads between steep hills and ridges of Capoocan and Limon, to cross towards the western side of the island, until they reach the gently downward rolling hills after Kanangga towards Ormoc. This topography was a dream scenario for those taking the high road or ambush positions and a nightmare for those below who are hemmed in by hills and ridges in some sections of the winding roads. It was also a disaster for heavy equipment who had to negotiate muddy roads. Most of the Leyte soil turned to bog during the rainy season.

Yamashita's troops in Leyte and Samar probably numbered less than half of the 160,000 American assault troops that landed by the end of October. They were now deployed in the hills of Capoocan and Carigara forming what they called the Yamashita's line. Their strategic objective was to delay the advance of the Americans and buy time for General Yamashita to consolidate his forces for the defense of Luzon. The Japanese reinforcements that quietly came from Manila and elsewhere started in 1943 as reported to Captain Yamaguchi by Major Inoue. But they were not enough compared with American forces that landed. The Japanese, it turned out, were outnumbered less than two is to one, out gunned and with practically no air cover. The Japanese troops did not stand a chance except for two things that were in their favor: the weather and the topography of the land. The weather greatly delayed the time-table of the advancing troops and made their progress painfully slow. General MacArthur's time table to reach Luzon had been greatly delayed. The battle had to be fought ridge after ridge on the way to Ormoc.

They were literally moving a few feet at a time through the bog and mud. The Japanese also occupied the high grounds along the narrow and winding road from Carigara to Capoocan. This was called the Pinamopoan-Ormoc Road while the Americans called it Highway 2. Breakneck Ridge crosses this road as one starts the climb from Carigara to Limon. *On this site, one of the bloodiest battles of the liberation of the Philippines will be fought.*

One of the company commanders assigned to defend the Breakneck Ridge was Captain Yamaguchi, formerly the commander of the Dulag garrison. Left for dead deep in a ravine after the ambush near the same site, Captain Yamaguchi although seriously wounded survived. The squad of Filipino guerillas who staged the treacherous assassination hurriedly left the scene when the first volley of fire felled Captain Yamaguchi and a couple of his men into the ravine. However, the six others were able to return fire and scatter their ambushers from both sides of the road. Fearing that Japanese reinforcements from nearby Kanangga and Ormoc would be alerted, the guerillas broke off and disappeared in the hills, confident that they have accomplished their mission – the assassination of Captain Yamaguchi. Luis

Borja was at the rear guard of the guerillas and one of those who saw Yamaguchi fall over the ravine. The rest of the Yamaguchi squad that included a medic were able to pull out Captain Yamaguchi from the ravine and applied first aid to the wounded officer. The two other soldiers were not so lucky. They absorbed most of the bullets that were intended for Yamaguchi. The survivors quietly proceeded to Kanangga where the Captain was given proper medical attention until he fully recovered at the Japanese camp in Ormoc. The Japanese intentionally kept the survival of Yamaguchi a secret for security reasons and because they had plans of pulling out of the Dulag garrison anyway. Based on this, even Luis thought that the captain was killed during the ambush.

Greatly disappointed and saddened by the betrayal, Yamaguchi realized that there was no such thing as friends or relatives during times of war. At least in his mind, Dalisay was not an exception. During the bloody American Civil war, relatives fought against relatives, friends against friends. Captain Yamaguchi took calculated risks and he almost lost. Still he did not think that

Dalisay would be capable of being a part of the dastardly act. This was also his way of dampening the hurt. The benefit of the doubt was all he could think of as he mused on what happened. As far as Mano Berto was concerned, it was all part of the game. But for Dalisay, it was simply beyond her ken. Yamaguchi, heartbroken as he was, still could not believe that his once beloved Dalisay could do this.

Just like Shakespeare's Romeo and Juliet, Yamaguchi and Dalisay's love affair was doomed right from the beginning. It became a tragedy caused by circumstances and missed opportunities. In Captain Yamaguchi's mind, his agony was worse than Dalisay's. What she must have felt when she learned of his alleged death was not comparable. Feeling betrayed by a loved one was far worse than being used, even for a noble cause. Like Dalisay, he felt anger in a different sense. Thin as it was often said, the boundary between his love and hate for Dalisay quickly dissolved. At least for a while. If he only knew. But still, he would not think of physically harming Dalisay. That would be too easy and kind for her. Maybe she deserved a more cruel punishment if guilty of the suspicion. Letting her know that he was alive should make her feel the burden of her evil did, if she were guilty, he pondered. She must know that she did not succeed. On the other hand, if she was not guilty, letting her know he was alive should be good for both of them. So, it was a win-win proposition. Like the guerillas, he too had Filipino assets to send and receive information. He now learned that Dalisay's parents did not survive the bombardment and that Dalisay was now under the care of the American liberators.

One rainy evening in November of 1944, after having cleared his mind and collected himself, he began to write a letter. He folded it carefully after he stamped it with his official signature. It was red, but not red ink. He used his own blood.

From the top of the Breakneck Ridge, Yamaguchi summoned his asset and asked him to send his letter to Dalisay in Palo.

"Please see to it that she gets this letter," Yamaguchi reminded the asset.

Bowing politely, the asset made an about-face and was quickly on his way even as the rain continued pouring.

The Montejo and Price Mansions

After Dalisay was discharged from the Palo, Infirmary, she was given a clerical work at the medical staff at the General Headquarters of General MacArthur at the Price Mansion in Tacloban. The supervisor of this staff was of course Macario Depuesto. Macario and Dalisay have grown closer to each other and the relationship became serious by the day. Although the last time Macario touched Dalisay was during her last physical therapy weeks earlier, the show of non-physical interaction belied the strong mutual affection that existed between the two. Unlike the Dulag garrison days, nothing had to be kept secret. Except for the superior-subordinate and ethical considerations at the workplace, there was nothing to stop the relationship from happening and growing. This time, there was no taboo.

The courtship was fast and like many couples during times of war, there was no time to waste. Barely a month from the time they met in the ward of the Palo, infirmary, Macario asked Dalisay to marry him. She said yes. They were married by Col. Ruperto Kangleon, the newly appointed Governor of Leyte, at their offices at the Price Mansion. MacArthur's wedding gift was his private suite at the Montejo Mansion for the honeymoon. Everything seemed so perfect until one day after their honeymoon.

When the Japanese forces occupied Tacloban, the Montejo Mansion was used as the headquarters of the Japanese commander of the occupying forces in Leyte. When the Americans landed in October 1944, the Montejos gladly offered it back to General Douglas MacArthur for his personal and official use. Meanwhile just two blocks away, at the corner of the present Sto. Nino and Justice Romualdez Streets, the Price Mansion, an elegant representative of American architecture for the wealthy of the 1900s, was used by Sergio Osmena and his Cabinet as the seat of power for the Commonwealth. It was built by Walter Scott Price, a native of Philadelphia, Pennsylvania. He was a member of the US Army assigned in the Philippines during the Spanish-American

War that ended in December 1898. He obtained an honorable dismissal from the army at the end of the Philippine-American war in 1901, after his last assignment which was Camp Bumpus in Tacloban. He married Simeona Kalingag from Cavite on January 1,1901 right after the war ended and built a palatial home in Tacloban for his wife and their 11 growing children. Walter Scott died on March 18, 1945 at the age of sixty-eight (68) years while Simeona, his wife, died on August 30, 1973, four and a half months after her one hundredth (100th) birthday. This was not an unusual occurrence for some of the soldiers who came to Samar and Leyte during the time of Gen. Arthur MacArthur, from 1900 to 1901. Some of them stayed and married the local women.

A Letter from Heaven or Hell?

The sun was finally out, Macario was still in bed while Dalisay was already busy preparing to hang the newly washed white linens, when the asset arrived at the Montejo mansion.

After making sure that no one else was with Dalisay, except Macario who was still in bed and sleeping in the room, the asset came to Dalisay and covertly handed the letter.

"Gin papahatag sa imo" said the asset and was preparing to leave (I was asked to give you this).

"Anay, hulat ka la. Hino man naghatag?" she said in waray. (Wait please. Who was the letter from?)

"Hi Yamaguchi", he replied at a low voice. "Secreto la" he continued. (From Yamaguchi and keep it secret.)

The moment she heard Yamaguchi, her face turned pale and she almost fainted.

"Buang ka! Kay buhi man siya?" Dalisay angrily asked after recovering. (Are you crazy, he is alive?)

"Basahin mo at sagutin mo yana" the asset replied. (Read it and answer it now if you wish.)

Dalisay began to open the folded letter and started reading.

"Dalisay San,

I do not know if you will be happy or sad because I am alive. Sorry, you and your fellow traitors did not succeed in killing me. You did not have to take all that trouble if that was all you wanted. You could have just poisoned me. Two of my loyal soldiers died and a couple of your guerillas were wounded. Their blood should be on you and your father's treachery. My only will to live now is to do my duty for my Emperor and my country. But do not worry because I will die soon but not by you or your father's hand. I will die in battle with my boots on. This is what I was trained for and I will gladly do so for my country and my Emperor. We will make this last stand here and I pray that the Divine Wind will take mine and my soldiers' spirits to heaven. I want you to know that more than the bullet, the hurt you inflicted in me was more painful.

But time heals everything. In fact, I have no more urge to take revenge. I am a soldier and you are only a woman. Soldiers fight with other soldiers. My only regret was that I protected you and your family because I thought you were real. I also know about your brother but I did not want you and your family harmed. Why then did I deserve what you did? Tell me please that you were not part of this!

I may never know your answer and why but there is one thing I am sure of. I am writing this not as a soldier but as someone who once loved another. I am glad that I will not have a chance to find whether our feelings for each other were the same. Please know that I am truly grateful for the times you shared with me at the camp. Those were the best times of my life. I forgive you and respect the choice that you made. I probably would have done the same if I were in your shoes. Country above self.

Sayonara.

Captain Yamaguchi

Japanese Imperial Army"

The Revelation

Macario was awakened by the sobs of Dalisay and got up to find out what was going on. Almost staggering, he found Dalisay curled at the foot and the corner of grand stairway leading to the second floor of the

Montejo mansion. By now he was really awake and his heart was pounding hard. He was preparing himself for the worse.

This was hard for someone or a couple who, just the night before were locked in passionate embrace and lovemaking. The last thing they needed the morning after was this aggravation. This was too exhausting mentally and emotionally.

“What is going on? What happened to you?” was all he could say upon seeing Dalisay. He did not notice yet the letter she was holding.

Noticing the courier, Macario became more aggressive and demandingly asked, “Who are you?”

Before Macario could turn more menacingly physical to the courier, Dalisay got up between Macario and the courier and said “Please stop. Let him go and I will explain to you.”

The courier was dismissed and obligingly retreated, out of sight of both Macario and Dalisay.

After recovering from the shock, Macario finally calmed down and sat down with Dalisay in their bedroom suite.

"Is there anything that I should worry about Dalisay? Better give it straight to me, while it is still early," Macario worriedly began to speak.

"I do not know how and where to begin but this has something to do with Captain Yamaguchi of the Dulag garrison," Dalisay replied calmly.

At this Macario lightened up but before he could speak another word, Dalisay continued and dropped the bombshell, "...and me."

Macario at this point was totally confused, dumbfounded and began to worry. He already knew that Dalisay's family was involved in intelligence gathering and were actually used as spies by the guerilla movement. Moreover, Dalisay and her brother were given credit for the assassination of Captain Yamaguchi. So, what could be the big fuss for Dalisay that brought her to her knees?

"What do you mean Captain Yamaguchi and ...you?" Macario asked.

"You did your job didn't you?" Macario continued to ask.

"Yes, I did," Dalisay replied bursting into tears while Macario stood up to hold her close in his arms.

"It is alright then. Why are you crying?" Macario reassured Dalisay as she continued to sob.

"He is alive and he sent me a letter," Dalisay replied between sobs.

At this, Macario replied, "Well then, that is not a problem. We will get him anyway because General Kruger's forces are on their way to Ormoc,". He said this to reassure Dalisay, not knowing yet what his wife was trying to tell him.

Dalisay at this point broke off from the embrace and started crying again. She took out the letter and showed it to Macario.

"You have to read this letter first and then I will explain it to you as your wife.

Promise me you will not get angry," she pleaded as she handed the letter.

Macario read and re-read the letter before he sat down again to talk to Dalisay.

With tears in his eyes and holding Dalisay's hand, he began to say, "Tell me this is not happening. Are you still in love with him? Am I now losing you just as fast as you came into my life?"

"No, please do not think that way my love," Dalisay replied, full of emotion and distress.

"I am now your wife and I intend to honor our vows. But we must put things right with Captain Yamaguchi. He had been really good to me and my family. He is an officer and a gentleman," Dalisay continued to reassure her husband.

"But are you still in love with him? I need to know," Macario protested.

"He was part of my past and that is where he belongs now. But I did not participate in his assassination. I would not be part of it anyway. My only concern now is to let him know that. At least he must know that I am not that kind of a person. He deserves to know the truth", Dalisay continued.

"So, what do you want to do now?" Macario asked.

"I want to send him a letter letting him know that I was not part of the plan and the assassination itself," Dalisay replied.

"It is only right that I ask for forgiveness, for me and my family," she continued.

"By now our forces will be surrounding their positions at Capoocan, but I will see what I can do," Macario replied, finally signifying his acceptance and support for Dalisay's request.

Dalisay started writing a note that would be brought to Captain Yamaguchi whose forces are now being besieged by General Kruger's pursuing forces at Limon, just 1,500 yards separating each other from the top of the Breakneck Ridge.

The Battle at Breakneck Ridge

The courier was escorted without any incident to the American front lines camped at Limon, along Pinamopoan-Ormoc Road. Macario who earned respect and distinction being a close-in aide of General MacArthur easily had his way around in facilitating the passage of the courier through the American pursuing forces until he reached the foot of the Breakneck Ridge where he was met by Japanese soldiers wielding white flags and proceeded to escort him up to the tent of Captain Yamaguchi. It was raining very hard and at the foot of the ridge, Sherman Tanks stuck in the mud have started pulverizing the top of the ridge. Mortar shells began to rain on the positions of the Japanese defenders who were hiding in their trenches and spider-holes. The courier handed his letter to Yamaguchi and asked to be dismissed immediately lest he was caught in the crossfire. Unfortunately, as soon as he stepped out of the tent, a shell exploded in front of him. It also took the life of one of his Japanese escorts that brought him to the camp.

Captain Yamaguchi started reading Dalisay's letter:

"Dear Yamaguchi Sama,

I am so glad that you are alive. I did not know that they planned to kill you. Had I known it beforehand, I would have warned you. Many of us from Dulag who are grateful to your kindness are praying for your safety.

I humbly ask for your forgiveness for me and my family.

I thought you were dead and I felt so desperate and lonely after I also lost my parents during the landing. I married a kind man who saved my life after I got seriously wounded. He is close to Gen. Douglas MacArthur. I was informed that your forces will not have a chance against their superior forces. They are just too many and you and your forces will perish if you fight. This time I do not want to lose you again. Please surrender and save your life and your soldiers too.

There is honor in surrendering. It is not cowardice to save your soldiers lives and your own. The Americans are just conquerors. My husband who is close to General MacArthur will see to it that you and your men will be treated fairly and well.

Please save your life. Surrender while there is still time

Sincerely,

DALISAY BORJA DEPUESTO"

Captain Yamaguchi, had a secret smile in his face after reading Dalisay's letter. Breathing a sigh of relief, he placed the letter in his left chest pocket.

Going out of his tent to rally his troops, he shouted, "Banzai Nippon!"

They in turn enthusiastically replied, "Banzai!"

The great battle at the Breakneck Ridge had begun in the earnest.

The first few days of the battle saw the Japanese inflicting heavy casualties to the attacking American forces because they had 30 caliber machinegun nests mounted on top of the ridge. Those were very efficient and lethal weapons. Wave after wave of assaults by the US X and XX Marine forces were repulsed by heavy fire from the top resulting in whole squads being wiped out. The battle was being waged inch-by-inch and foot-by-foot from the Limon position of the Americans to the top of the Breakneck Ridge. After more than a week of relentless pounding on the Japanese, the Americans were still 1,000 yards from the Japanese position, from their starting point at 1,500 yards. With bayonets fixed, both protagonists prepared for a hand-to-hand combat.

The Americans struck the Japanese defenders with everything they had – tanks, flamethrowers, mortars, Thompson submachine guns (TSMGs), Browning Automatic Rifles (BAR) and 105 mm artillery howitzers. But the Japanese still tenaciously held their positions on top of the ridge. Then the weather cleared and the bombers from the carriers and nearby Tacloban airfield were called in. It took several bomb-runs and strafing before the Japanese machine gun nests were silenced. This was the signal for the attacking troops to storm the top. With bayonets fixed, fierce-hand-to hand combat ensued. The Americans simply overwhelmed the outnumbered and outgunned troops of Captain Yamaguchi. But they held on for as long as they could because after the fall of Breakneck Ridge, there was nothing that will stop the Americans from proceeding to Ormoc. The road will be flatter and a lot easier to negotiate after the Breakneck Ridge.

Captain Yamaguchi was ready and waiting. Closing his eyes as if praying, he asked his aide to be ready as well.

“Captain sir, do you want me to assist you?” the aide asked. He was thinking that the Captain will now commit “hara-kiri” just like his samurai ancestors did generations before. That was the honorable thing to do.

“There’s no time for that,” the Captain told the aide as he held on to his pistol and waved away his aide. Hara-kiri if performed was an elaborate ritual that usually required the help of an aide, in the case of important persons like Captain Yamaguchi.

“Try to live so you can tell my family and the Emperor what we did here. Go now!” the Captain said in a hurry.

Captain Yamaguchi was among the last to be killed being an officer. He held his post at his tent with his pistol in hand and was confronted by two American soldiers who immediately recognized him as the commanding officer of the Japanese forces.

Aiming their M-1 rifles at the Captain, one of the soldiers yelled, “In the name of the US Armed Forces, bring down your weapon and surrender!”

“Banzai Nippon!” Captain Yamaguchi shouted in reply and began to raise and aim his pistol at them.

Two bullets tore through the Captain’s heart and through the letter in his chest pocket even before he could raise his pistol to fire at the soldiers. He was among the last of the 5,252 Japanese soldiers who lost their lives in this battle. Together with the Japanese dead was the body of the courier who brought the letter of Dalisay to the Captain. On the American side, 1,498 soldiers paid with their lives for every inch of the 1,500 yards that they gained at Breakneck Ridge.

CHAPTER 9

Post War Life of the Depuestos and Asis'

"War destroys as well as it creates. Time heals the wound, but scars remain. We forgive but still not forget."

The Japanese surrendered to the Americans in the Philippines on September 3, 1945 at Camp John Hay, Baguio City. General Tomoyuki Yamashita formally surrendered in the presence of high-ranking American officers, including General Wainwright, the American General who surrendered to the Japanese in Bataan on April 9, 1942.

To prevent the death of more innocent civilians and further destruction of Tokyo, Japan, the Japanese Emperor Hirohito announced Japan's surrender on August 15, 1945 shortly after the Americans dropped the first two atomic bombs ever used during the war, the one *Enola Gay* dropped at Hiroshima and the other one that was dropped at Nagasaki. The destruction and death were instantaneous but the damage and harm would last for decades as it took time for the radioactive infection to decay and subside. This was the validation of the success of America's Manhattan Project at UC Berkeley. America was first to invent and use a weapon of mass destruction that could literally end life on earth as we know it. The Empire of Japan paid very dearly for their military adventurism and their dream of a *Great East Asia Prosperity Sphere.*

On board the US battleship USS Missouri, the flag ship of the American Naval forces for the conquest of Japan, the Japanese representatives of the Imperial family and the Japanese government signed formally the instrument of surrender on September 2, 1945. Thus, ended the world's bloodiest and most destructive war with nearly 2,000,000 Japanese dead and about 200,000 allied forces and civilians killed. Half of these Pacific War casualties were Americans, and about 30,000 of the dead were Filipino soldiers.

These did not include the thousands of civilians who were killed by the panicking and retreating Japanese forces. Thousands more of innocent Filipino civilians were killed not by the enemy bullets but by American bombs. The carpet bombing by American B-24s of population centers where there were suspected Japanese camps and garrisons caused the loss of whole generations of Filipino families. Over-all, American bombs in 1945 killed more Filipinos than the Japanese did from December 1941 to their surrender in the Philippines on September, 1945.

The immediate goal on hand after the surrender of Japan as far as Gen. Douglas MacArthur was concerned was how to win the minds of the Japanese people and complete the conquest and conversion of Japan into a peace-time nation. Prior to this defeat, Japan was ruled and run by militarists and war-hawks that turned the nation into a military state. The once formidable Japanese Imperial Army owed absolute allegiance and loyalty to the Emperor. The Japanese people who once believed that their emperor descended from the Gods were equally loyal and would die for the emperor. It was the thinking of Gen. MacArthur that they could only effectively transform the post-war Japanese government and society with the help and cooperation of the Imperial family who still commanded great respect and loyalty from the Japanese people. The Imperial throne had to be saved.

Immediately after the war, the allied countries were intent to prosecute the war criminals of the Second World War, particularly the German war criminals who were responsible for implementing Adolf Hitler's "Final Solution" of the Jewish question. There were those who believed that the same effort must be expended to prosecute the Japanese war criminals at the Pacific theatre of the war. David Bergamimi in his book "The Great Imperial Conspiracy" implicated the imperial family with "direct complicity" in the conduct of the war by the

Japanese. Bergamimi suggested that the Japanese Imperial family was culpable in the war atrocities committed by the Japanese forces against the US and its Pacific allies. But Gen. MacArthur who was given the responsibility of "rehabilitating and converting" post-war Japan had a problem with this. To MacArthur, the people of Japan had suffered enough and the priority at hand was to rebuild Japan and never again allow it to become a war-like nation that it had been. He was determined to save the imperial family from being tried for war crimes, if only to effectively govern a country of fanatic citizens who believed that their emperor was indeed a "sun-god".

For this reason, General MacArthur had to hold court in Tokyo immediately following the surrender of Japan to implement his grand rehabilitation plan. This was how Japan rose from the ashes of defeat to become one of the largest economies of the world after the Second World War.

Post-War Depuesto Family Life

Macario Depuesto in the meantime decided to stay behind in Manila, where there were also a lot of post-war rebuilding, not to mention the fact that he was starting a family of his own. They had all the reasons to stay. They had relatives up north in Ilocos and in Tacloban, Leyte. Macario had connections to the very top of Philippine bureaucracy as well as the American occupiers after the war.

Macario and Dalisay Depuesto settled in Manila to be near the US Embassy, Macario's place of work. They also bought a family farm in Sta. Maria, Ilocos Sur which they used as their second home. Macario and Dalisay Depuesto's marriage was blessed by four children, the eldest of which was a girl born less than a year after the war, on July 4, 1946. They named her Julia in honor of their grandfather Julian and because she was born on July 4th, 1946 when the Philippines was given political independence by the Americans. After a long fight for independence that was started by Manuel L. Quezon as first President of the Philippine Commonwealth in 1935, the efforts by his successors Sergio Osmena and Manuel Roxas finally bore fruit. Macario was honorably discharged from the military in 1946 but opted to work at the American Embassy along

Dewey Boulevard (now Roxas Boulevard) and near the Manila Hotel, the favorite and second home of MacArthur in Manila.

Life has never been better for the Depuestos. General MacArthur made sure that Macario got a good job at the US Embassy, working as a civilian attaché for the US military. In Manila, Macario got to rub elbows with Manila's 400 and the powers that be in Malacañang and the newly organized Philippine legislature. He was on first name basis with General Carlos P. Romulo and former President Sergio Osmena of the Philippine Commonwealth. Even at the US embassy in Manila, he was held in high esteem by the Americans because of his service during the war and his close connection with General MacArthur. He carried one of the highest levels of security clearance given to high ranking American and Filipino officers who served at the USAFFE. Every now and then, he would be sent to Washington D.C. for an official mission but no sooner than when he got there, he would wish that he was back in Manila.

The reason was simple. In the US, Macario was still considered a second-class citizen, because of his ethnicity. Although he grew up in Hawaii, and became a naturalized American citizen, he did not have the “right” color or complexion. This was still the late 40s and 50s, long before the Civil Rights Movement broke some barriers in the US mainstream society. He would however not deny his heritage because he had always been open about his family’s origins. Besides, he could not deny his Filipino heritage and ties that opened the door for him to the Philippine high society, the high and the mighty in Philippine bureaucracy and politics. It was much better and more advantageous for him as an American, to live in the Philippines than to go back to America where he was treated like any other ordinary Asian immigrant to America. He decided to make the Philippines his home.

Julia was followed by another sibling, this time a boy named Macario Jr., while the third was another boy named Douglas, a namesake of his former boss, General MacArthur. The youngest was Ligaya who was born in 1962, a menopause baby. While Macario spoke English without an accent, all his children were born in Manila and grew up with other Filipino boys and girls and therefore spoke English with deep Ilocano accent. They in fact spoke Tagalog and Ilocano at home in Sta. Maria Ilocos Sur. Ligaya in particular grew up in Sta. Maria, Ilocos Sur, Macario and Dalisay's postal address in the Philippines.

Julia immigrated to Hawaii against her father's wishes and married an Ilocano, who was born and raised in Hawaii. Macario Jr. and Douglas joined the US army and likewise settled in Hawaii. Ligaya was left alone with her parents, who were determined to keep her in Manila. But at age 18 and with the vehemence of the Hollywood culture in Manila that depicted America as the modern version of the biblical land of "milk and honey", Ligaya began to dream of going to America herself. Macario as an American citizen who served as a regular serviceman in the USAFFE during the Second World War, with a high-level security clearance enjoyed some perks and privileges from the American government. One of these was the privilege to petition his family members on priority basis to become permanent residents and later on become American citizens. He deliberately kept this information to himself in the case of his youngest daughter Ligaya. Both Macario and Dalisay thought that Ligaya will do just as well if not better in Manila, considering their station in society and connections in the Philippines.

But Ligaya would not be denied. Ligaya although the youngest, was the most independent and adventurous among the siblings. Unlike her parents, Ligaya was born to an above average Filipino-American family. Financially, they were well off with Macario's back pay, military pension and his salary at the US embassy. Ligaya inherited Macario's genes as far as her ambition, persistence and attitude in life were. She was most inquisitive of what her dad actually did and why he was close to the famous American war hero, General Douglas MacArthur. She was determined to find out and go to America, one way or another.

Eventually she did get to know who her dad was and how her grandfather, without a penny, migrated to the US through the plantations of Hawaii. Macario and Dalisay realized the futility of making Ligaya stay in Ilocos. The very first week after her 18th birthday, she was on board a Philippine Airlines plane on her way to Honolulu, Hawaii to join her Ate Julia.

Ligaya Depuesto, 3rd Generation Filipino-American

As soon as Ligaya settled in Honolulu Hawaii at her Ate Julia's house, she prepared to make sure she gets into college. She was now a permanent US resident of Honolulu, Hawaii and an American citizen. The Ilocanos in Hawaii were of different breed from the rest of Filipino-Americans who migrated to America. First of all, they were closely knit and brought their own family customs and traditions and culture in Hawaii. They have every reason to be proud because they were the descendants of the First-generation Filipinos who migrated to America through Hawaii who have gone a long way from just being farms workers to becoming prosperous and respected citizens of Hawaii. They want to call themselves Ilocano more than being called Filipino. Ligaya therefore blended pretty well with the Ilocano-Americans (Filipino-Americans) of Hawaii.

Ligaya got the genes of her father physically, emotionally and intellectually. She was outspoken and quite naturally proud of who she was. This was because of her father's background and credentials with the American government. She was fairer and taller than the average Ilocano lasses both in Ilocos and in Honolulu. She had a pleasing personality and was a natural go-getter. She eventually finished her degree in Political Science at the East-West University of Hawaii and became a naturalized American citizen.

Again, using her father's credentials and connection, Ligaya landed a federal job in Honolulu, at the office of the Department of State. Most Filipino-Americans in Honolulu, just like California were Democrats. But Ligaya's own beliefs aligned more with the Republican platform. Besides, she got her job from a Republican friend, a former Ambassador to the Philippines. She was active in the community and she enjoyed her work at the Department of State. She too had her own security clearance from the Department of State. Part of her job was to monitor the political developments in her community and even from the Philippines that might have a bearing on American foreign policy among other federal government matters. Everything seemed to naturally happen and fall into place. Ligaya was on her way to fully exploit her potential in Hawaii and the US mainland.

The Baby-boomers and Post-War American Economy

By fall of 1945, thousands of American soldiers started coming back home to America. The baby-boom started in the earnest when the war ended. New settlements outside the big cities called the suburbs sprouted like mushrooms all over the eastern and western seaboard. Big cities had to make room for thousands of new and growing American families. The Americans started building its great highway system right after the war, opening new residential areas. The vaunted American industrial might was now directed to building America, not just their military. Factories were humming with the production of peace time products like cars and appliances. Construction and home-building were among the fastest growing industries. After the second world war,

Americans can easily buy a ranch type house for less than $10,000. The same ranch houses would sell to the wealthy middleclass Americans forty years later for ten to twenty times its original value in the 1940s in the San Francisco, Bay area. Peacetime was good but there was still anxiety on the "red or yellow menace" as Communist Russia and China were both identified as threats to the democracies of the free world and enemies of capitalism. The so called "Cold war" would begin immediately with the division of Berlin into the West (under the US authority) and East Berlin (under the Russian authority).

The Asis Family Settles in Vallejo, Northern California

Arnulfo Asis was now retired and settled in Vallejo California, a bustling town 35 miles northeast of San Francisco, just north of the Carquinez Strait. This is how Wikipedia described the City of Vallejo:

"The present City of Vallejo is located on the southwestern edge of what is now known as Solano County, California in the North Bay region of the San Francisco Bay Area in

Northern California. Vallejo is accessible by Interstate-80 that runs east to west, between Sacramento and San Francisco.

The northern half of the Carquinez Bridge is anchored in Vallejo. It can also be reached by Interstate 780 from neighboring Benicia to the east, and by Route 37 from Marin County to the west. Route 29 (former U.S. Route 40) begins in the city near the Carquinez Bridge and travels north through the heart of the city and beyond into, Napa County, entering the neighboring American Canyon and eventually, Napa. Vallejo borders the present city of Benicia to the east, American Canyon and the Napa county line to the north, the Carquinez Strait to the south and the San Pablo Bay to the west."

According to the same source, "the City of Vallejo was once part of the 84,000-acre (340 km^2) Rancho Suscol Mexican land grant of 1843 by Governor Manuel Micheltorena to Gen. Mariano Guadalupe Vallejo. The city was named after this Mexican military officer and title holder who was appointed in settling and overseeing the north bay region. General Vallejo was responsible for military peace in the region and founded the pueblo of Sonoma in 1836. In 1846 independence-minded Anglo immigrants rose up against the Mexican government of California in what would be known as the Bear Flag Revolt which resulted in his imprisonment at Sutter's Fort."

Following this event, California was annexed to the United States. General Vallejo, though a Mexican army officer, was very open and cooperative to the annexation of California to the United States, because "he recognized the greater resources of the United States and benefits that it would bring to California." The Americans naturally liked General Vallejo because he was "a proponent of reconciliation and statehood after the Bear Flag Revolt." He was so popular to the Americans that a U.S. Navy submarine, the USS *Mariano G. Vallejo* (SSBN-658), was even named after him.

According to historical records, the man regarded as the true founder of Vallejo was an American named John B. Frisbie. After General Vallejo's daughter Epifania married Frisbie, he granted Frisbie a power of attorney for the land grant. It was Frisbie who hired E.H. Rowe, the man who designed the city layout and who named the east-west streets after states and the north-south streets after California counties.

The US government set up its first Naval Shipyard in the 1850s at Mare Island, in Vallejo. It was called the Mare Island Naval Shipyard or MINSY. Sustained by a large US Naval ship yard, Vallejo became a boom-town for most of the 1900s up to the 1960s.

It was the place to be for those who are serving and those who served the US military. This was home to the famed Nautilus, the nuclear-powered sub who used to visit the Philippines secretly to send medical supplies, relay and receive information from the Filipino resistance in the Visayas and Mindanao.

CHAPTER 10

Loreto Asis, 3rd Generation Fil-Am

"You are not a Filipino!"

Upon his honorable discharge from the military, Arnulfo came back to Vallejo and married an Italian American and a longtime resident of Vallejo and begot a son they named Loreto.

With the US Naval shipyard at Mare Island still very busy, Vallejo thrived as one of the fast-growing cities in northern California, outside of San Francisco and Oakland. This was the city where Loreto grew up, in a community of Italian Americans in Vallejo. He attended Vallejo High school and graduated as valedictorian of class 1965. Unlike the Depuestos who lived with fellow Ilocanos and other immigrants in California, the Asis family lived with Italian Americans in Vallejo and Loreto had no direct social interaction with Filipinos until later. This was deliberate on the part of Arnulfo. He told his son that he should avoid associating with Filipinos, African Americans and Latinos, for fear of being discriminated against. They made good friends with everyone except with Filipinos. But it was hard for young Loreto to miss them. They were in the public schools, the community Town Hall meetings and even in UC Berkeley near Oakland. UC Berkeley is one of the two ivy league universities in northern California. The other university, its rival since the 1800s was the Stanford University in Palo Alto, at the peninsula of the Bay Area.

"You are not a Filipino!"

Fresh from high school and graduating at the top of his class, Loreto was going over the application forms for UC Berkeley. Loreto noticed that in all the application forms he had filled up, his parents ticked the box for American citizens. But now the UC Berkeley form had an additional line for "Ethnic Origin".

The choices were: "Hawaiian and South Pacific Islanders, Latino, Chinese and other Asians".

"Which one are we dad?", Loreto asked his dad.

"Definitely not Other Asians and Filipinos.", Arnulfo snapped at his son.

"Dad, there is no box for Filipinos!" Loreto corrected his dad. "Well, I am sure we are not Chinese or even Latinos. Should I check the box for Hawaiian and Pacific Islanders or Other Asians?", he continued to ask.

After hesitating for a moment, Arnulfo replied, "That's the one, Hawaiian or Pacific Islanders. Your grandfather and I came from there."

Arnulfo deliberately omitted the fact that his father and mother actually were natives of Pagudpud, Ilocos Norte and Taft, Eastern Samar. As far as he was concerned, this was not important for Loreto to know. It was only as late as the 80s when schools in mainland America included Filipinos in the list of "Ethnic Origins". Before this time, Filipinos were lumped with the Pacific Islanders.

Paradigm Shift in American Politics and Society

After Democratic President Harry Truman left the Whitehouse in the 1950s, the popular commander of the American and Allied forces of the war at the European theatre, Gen. Dwight Eisenhower was elected to office as President of the U.S. Just like in the Roman Empire, in great civilizations and countries like the US, leaders emerge and become recognized following great military conquests. Eisenhower rose to the seat of American power via a similar route that Julius Caesar of Rome did. However, this will not be the same for General Douglas MacArthur. This true "American Caesar" would simply "fade away" after the war, content with just being remembered as a true and professional soldier.

As late as in Eisenhower's second term, Dr. Martin Luther King, Jr. would be making a name for himself, launching what would later be known as the Civil Rights Movement of America. In 1960, a young charismatic and Catholic Senator from Boston, Massachusetts would be elected to the Whitehouse, Sen. John F. Kennedy and will place the Civil Rights movement as one of his flagship initiatives. Kennedy, a Democrat, was determined to end segregation and fight racism in America. But Lee Harvey Oswald abruptly ended this quest when he fired the fatal bullets to President Kennedy's head as he passed the public library building in Dallas, Texas in November, 1963.

Loreto at this time was a full scholar at UC Berkeley at the College of Engineering. UC Berkeley in Northern California was a hot bed for student activism just like Sorbonne University was in Sorbonne, France. There were student demonstrations almost every week at the Berkeley campus protesting against segregation and racial discrimination. Loreto could not help but be in a few of these student protests but just as a bystander.

During one of these protest meetings, Loreto chanced upon a group of Asian scholars (Chinese and Filipino scholars) mulling a plan to join their African American brothers in a rally against segregation and racial discrimination.

"Hey Larry, why don't you join us in our next protest rally? Aren't you Filipino also?" asked one of the Filipino scholars who accosted Loreto.

"Well, I would love to, but I am not really a Filipino. I am a Hawaiian and I need to study your issues first," he politely replied.

To this reply the Filipino fellows looked at each other in wonderment.

“Oh, but you looked like one of us,” the other Filipino student quipped.

“No. Sorry,” Loreto replied as he quickly left the group.

That evening, Loreto could not help but think about that brief encounter with a couple of Filipino and Chinese scholars in UC Berkeley. He wanted to ask his father a few questions but remembering his father’s reminders about who they were, he stopped and decided to continue working on his readings in “Structural Engineering”.

Loreto was taking up Bachelor of Science in Civil Engineering but he was equally interested and attracted to Electrical Engineering as well. Thus, he would spend hours reading electrical engineering books on top of his regular readings and assignments on Civil Engineering. He was particularly interest on how “photo voltaic” technology worked. Photo voltaic is another name for electrical energy generated from photo voltaic cells, or solar energy cells. This technology was for years used by the military and developed under the auspices of the National Aeronautics and Space Agency (NASA). UC Berkeley would prominently figure in the development of the world's first Atomic bomb under the top-secret Manhattan Project at its Lawrence Livermore laboratories at the Berkeley hills and Livermore, California. This was the reputation and environment that scientists and students of engineering in UC were exposed to. At UC Berkeley, protected by the quest for science and technology, scientists working on the *Manhattan Project*, were shielded from racial discrimination. It was greatly minimized if ever. One's worth is valued according to one's contribution to science and technology. Loreto particularly liked this concept and was driven by it.

The First Filipino-American Elected to Public Office

Loreto survived the chaotic student activism that UC Berkeley was known for and graduated with distinction as a Civil Engineer. Many offers came his way because this was the period of uninterrupted post-war expansion of the American economy. Many

American companies were growing very fast and were reaping America's leading position as a world power. Militarily, America had extended its military might with bases built in Southeast Asia, Europe and even in Saudi Arabia. America's market for its goods and services were the whole continent of Europe and its former colonies or protectorates in Asia like the Philippines, Japan, Taiwan and Korea. Bechtel Company was also growing as fast as the economy would allow it, with the massive postwar building requirements in Europe, Japan and the rest of Asia. Loreto became one of the leading civil engineers of Bechtel Company that was based in San Francisco, California.

In no time, Loreto became one of the Vice Presidents of the Company in his early 30s. In the late 60s and 70's this was significant because although Loreto was considered a natural-born American, his father Arnulfo and his grandfather Manoling descended from an ethnic minority, namely Filipino. Although Loreto and his father Arnulfo did not particularly flaunt this, it was obvious from his appearance (brown, stocky and black hair) that he was different from the other vice presidents of the company who were white and generally blond or brown hair. His case was a rare example of an Asian-American, of ethnic origin breaking through the "glass ceiling".

In his 20s, young and successful, Loreto became the young favorite not only among the Italian American community in Vallejo, but also the Filipino-American community that was also fast growing in the same city. The two communities would take Loreto for their own and Loreto would easily win a seat in City Council of Vallejo. Although Arnulfo would not identify with the Filipino-Americans, he tolerated it at best for the sake of politics. Politics was addition. Loreto's inclination was with the Democrats whose vision and mission were more people centered than the Republicans.

At least this was how Loreto viewed the Democrats. Loreto will rapidly rise among the ranks of the young and dynamic leaders of the Democratic Party in the City of Vallejo. As soon as he was elected councilor, the Filipino-Americans in Vallejo proudly adopted Loreto as their own. The city council would elect from their ranks the mayor of the city on a rotation basis. And soon enough, it was Loreto's turn and he became Mayor of Vallejo before he turned 30. He did not know it at that time but as far as the Filipino-American constituents of Vallejo were concerned, Loreto was recognized as the first Filipino-American ever elected in a public office and the first to become mayor of an American city.

Loreto would marry Sonia, a former classmate at UC Berkeley and they would have a daughter named Apolonia, in keeping with the Italian American heritage of her mother. This time, the Asis genes were over-powered by the Italian American genes as Apolonia took her mother's brown curly, hair, long eyelashes, brown eyes and fair skin.

Eventually, Loreto and Sonia would take their prominent place in the community as respected and successful UC Berkeley graduates. Loreto's job at Bechtel would bring him to different projects of the company all over Europe and sometimes Asia. Apolonia would practically grow up without really bonding with his father Loreto. Eventually the matter of raising Apolonia properly became a major issue in the family as Loreto would rather have Sonia quit her job and take care of Apolonia full-time. But Sonia was not going to be just a housewife that Loreto wanted her to be. Besides, Loreto had difficulty in bringing Sonia to his side of the family as she could not relate. The Asis family all looked different from Sonia's family. They soon found themselves drifting away from each other. Just as Apolonia was turning 17, they decided that it will be best for the child and for all of them to separate ways. The divorce was finalized but not after some acrimonious settlement of conjugal properties. Sonia took custody of Apolonia, and half of Loreto's assets.

As years passed, Loreto became more popular in the community and became more deeply involved in politics. Sonia and Loreto had to mend their relationship, became friends again at least for the sake of Apolonia and the public.

CHAPTER 11

The Rise of Filipino-American Empowerment

"Consequently, when an Asian breaks the so-called glass ceiling whether at work, business or politics, just like Loreto Asis did, it made a lot of noise.."

By the late 1980s and early 1990s, Filipino-Americans became one of the fastest growing ethnic minorities all over the US, from Hawaii, California, Nevada, Texas, Chicago, New Jersey, New York and Florida. A close third behind the Latinos and the Chinese, the influx of the first, second and third generation Filipino-Americans during the last 50 years began to be felt by mainstream America in politics and the economy. Filipinos were also the largest group that were easily assimilated into the mainstream, among the immigrant ethnic minorities.

The US Census of 2000 and 2010

One of the eye-opening revelations of the US Census of population among Asians and the American white population in 2000 and 2010 was that the *Asian population increased more than four times faster than the total U.S. population.* The Census Bureau reported that the total U.S. population grew by only 9.7 percent, from 281.4 million in 2000 to 308.7 million in 2010. *In comparison, the Asian alone population increased more than four times faster than the total U.S. population, growing by 43 percent from 10.2 million to 14.7 million.* In the same report, it was revealed that the Asian alone-or-in-combination population experienced slightly more growth than the Asian alone population, growing by 46 percent from 11.9 million in

2000 to 17.3 million in 2010. The report indicated that the observed changes in the race counts between Census 2000 and the 2010 Census could be attributed to a number of factors. Demographic change since 2000, which includes births and deaths in a geographic area and migration in and out of a geographic area. The report also said that some changes in the race question's wording and format since Census 2000 could have influenced reporting patterns in the 2010 Census.

Filipinos are Second only to the Chinese-Americans in Population Count

According to the same Census report of 2000 and 2010 by the US Census Bureau, Filipinos were now the second largest Asian group in the United States. The number of Americans who have identified themselves as Filipino, either alone or in combination with another race, totaled 3.4 million, the report showed. However, the total number is believed to be much higher than the census count because there were an estimated one million undocumented Filipinos in the United States.

Chinese-Americans made up the largest Asian group, with more than 4 million. Those from the Indian subcontinent were the third largest, with 3.2 million. Other significantly large Asian groups included the Vietnamese, with 1.7 million; Koreans, with 1.7 million, and the Japanese, with 1.3 million.

This statistical profile was based on the 2010 census of major racial and ethnic groups in the United States. Released on March 22, 2018 the statistical portrait of the Asian-American and Native Hawaiian and Pacific Islander populations were produced for the Asian Pacific American Heritage Month, which was celebrated annually.

This census period covered part of the so called 4th Filipino-American Generation. This specifically includes all Filipino-Americans born after 1997. This classification, by the way, actually coincides or conforms with Michael Dimock's (of Pew Research Center) classification tool for the Post-Millennial generation.

The growth in numbers of Asians, including our so called Fourth generation Filipino-Americans may not be as impactful to the mainstream American society as the third and earlier generations of Filipino-Americans were. The reasons for this were many.

For instance, the first and second-generation Filipino-Americans were not assimilated into the mainstream American society because of the prevailing social and political barriers that prevented them from doing so. Segregation, racial discrimination and non-acceptance of mixed marriages were the main reasons. Filipinos, just like other ethnic immigrants like the Chinese will tend to form their own racial and social enclaves where they felt safe, secure and accepted. The good side of this was that they brought with them their old customs and traditions, family and cultural values that enriched the multifaceted culture and melting pot that is the American society today. They may be less in numbers but their contribution to the American way of life via their distinctively Asian cultural art, music, food and customs and traditions have enriched the American way of life. Their retention of their own culture and way of life was an addition to and an enrichment of the already pluralistic American society and culture.

Secondly, because they were generally discriminated against, it was difficult for the earlier Filipino Immigrants to get assimilated. It was even harder to get ahead economically. Most of the jobs opened to them were menial if not low paying jobs. These are jobs that the white Americans do not want. There were no equal opportunity employers and opportunities as well. Not until Martin Luther King's Civil Rights movement finally broke through in the late 60s and 70s. These were the generations where the Loretos and Ligayas of the Third generation Filipino-American immigrants were born into. At least there were laws passed to level the playing field, socially and economically.

By the late 1970s, racial discrimination had been generally outlawed. Companies were encouraged to become equal opportunity employers. Incentives were given to companies and businesses who will employ women and minorities. These gains of minorities and African Americans in their social and political rights were the outcomes of the Civil Rights movement that the Democratic Party strongly supported. Consequently, when an Asian breaks the so-called glass ceiling whether at work, business or politics, just like Loreto Asis did, it made a lot of noise. It got the attention of mainstream America.

Last but not least, those born from Filipino-American families from 1997 to the present, including those who became Americans through immigration, were easily assimilated into the American mainstream society. The social, racial and political barriers that prevented the earlier generations of Filipino-Americans from getting assimilated into the mainstream society were all but neutralized, if not eliminated by affirmative action and anti-discrimination laws. They were also educated and more affluent than their First and Second-generation predecessors.

Today political correctness is the norm. This meant saying the right things and avoiding the labelling of minorities, especially women. Mixed marriages and interracial relationships were no longer taboo. The

Asians especially took great strides in economic and political empowerment. When Asians (including Filipinos) do get assimilated, they lose their unique identifiers as Asian Americans or Filipino-Americans. They simply blend in and become part of the mainstream American society that has also drastically evolved and transformed to its present profile, the new American, the Post-Millennial American. He or she is no longer white, blonde or blue eyed. He could be black, brown, yellow or a combination of races. This was what Mutya Asis was born into. She was an example of the new American, a product of mixed races, not necessarily white but a natural-born American.

Filipino-American Republicans and Democrats

California had always been a Democratic Party dominated state. This is because the largest population of ethnic minorities reside in this state. The top three ethnic minorities in terms of population after 2010 were the Chinese, Filipinos and Latinos in that order. These three comprised the majority of the ethic population of California.

The Democrats had been the champion of government funded entitlements for minorities in the US. Their biggest cities, Los Angeles and San Francisco had been declared as “havens for undocumented immigrants”.

In the eyes of a few Filipino-American Republicans like Ligaya Depuesto, these were entitlements that do not foster self-reliance and hard-work. Being a hardworking Filipino-American herself, Ligaya believed that America was built by strong, hardworking and self-reliant people, not those who depended on government aid and support to survive. Ligaya supported the Filipino-American communities but she did not want them to be public wards, dependent on government dole-outs.

Loreto on the other hand welcomed the populist policies and initiatives of the Democratic Party. As a politician Loreto believed that he could get more votes by supporting the Democratic pro-poor and populist social initiatives. Loreto now realized that it was in fact an advantage to be identified and become part of the Filipino-American community. If only his dad lived long enough to witness this, he probably would openly acknowledge his Filipino heritage. Arnulfo died of cancer of the lungs in 2001. By then, Loreto had openly welcomed the support from his Filipino-American friends who would take him as their own. He continued to maintain his ties with his Italian-American relatives, friends and their mainstream American allies. This was good politics among the Third and Fourth generation Filipino-Americans.

In the 90s, more and more Filipino-Americans would be elected into public office from Hawaii, Northern and Southern California, Chicago, Illinois and other states where the Filipino-American population had grown significantly to make a difference in local elections. They were either a major group to contend with or at the very least, the swing votes during close political contests. The Third generation Filipino-Americans produced a lot of professionals like doctors, nurses, engineers, architects, lawyers, entrepreneurs and college graduates.

The Veterans Equity Bill of 1997

One of the major initiatives that significantly contributed to the rise of

Filipino-American empowerment was the fight for the Veterans Equity Bill that started around August 1997 when the various Filipino-American Associations all over America and the Hawaiian Islands gathered in Washington D.C. to form the National Federation of Filipino-American Associations (NaFFAA). This became the umbrella organization of all Filipino-American associations in the US mainland and the Hawaiian Islands. NaFFAA became the voice of Filipino-Americans in the US Capitol. Their maiden and flagship initiative was to lobby for the passing of the Veterans Equity Bill that became a law during the term of President Clinton. The timing was right during Clinton's term when the country experienced an unprecedented continuous economic growth and expansion. In addition, America had both a Democratic President and Congress in power. The Veterans Equity Bill was a law that was passed in order to rectify an injustice by the American government to the Filipino veterans who fought alongside with the Americans through the USAFFE, before and during the Second World War and the liberation of the Philippines. After the war, the American government unjustly withdrew the recognition of Philippine guerillas and Filipino war veterans for the purpose of denying them full payment of US veterans benefits enjoyed by regular American servicemen who served during the war. It took NaFFAA more than 15 years to win it but it was more than just a political victory for the Filipino-American lobbyists. It was an affirmation of and the recognition of the growing Filipino-American political empowerment in the US.

This was one of the main reasons why Loreto became attracted to Filipino-American issues and politics. He was one of the charter members of NaFFAA in Washington D.C. in 1997. Ligaya attended the three-day conference as an observer for the Department of State. It was interesting for her because she had friends and relatives who would benefit from this initiative. But she and her family were not directly affected or benefitted by the law because her dad Macario was already a recognized regular US Army veteran and a full-fledged American citizen before, during and after the war. Besides, his position as a close-in Medical Aide-De-Camp of General MacArthur gave her father a lot more benefits than any ordinary World War II veteran.

The Chance Meeting at the Conference

On the second day of the conference, a grand Dinner Fellowship was held for the delegates at the grand ball room of Hilton Hotel where most of the delegates were billeted. Among the attendees were Ligaya Depuesto who joined the Hawaiian delegation, while Loreto joined the Vallejo Fil-American Democrats delegation of the San Francisco Bay Area Fil-Am Associations.

Loreto who was a very illegible bachelor at this time saw Ligaya at the corner of his eye. She was at least twelve years younger but definitely a very eligible bachelorette herself.

"May I have the pleasure of this dance?" the young Democrat from Vallejo asked Ligaya as he extended his hands to the young lady.

As they danced the night away, there were questions in the eyes of other dancers on the floor but only Loreto and Ligaya knew the answers. There were witty verbal exchanges about each other's political affiliation, with each trying to out-smart the other. But there were also exchanges of mutual admiration and respect. In fact, one would have a hard time deciding who really was flirting with whom. They flirted with each other.

Being a politician, Loreto's background and reputation had been an open book. Ligaya knew it all but she also wanted to get to know this Democrat better and face-to-face. Part of it was her adventurous nature and partly to challenge this Democrat and perhaps convert him to become a Republican. Poor Loreto, Ligaya had a complete background information on him while he did not really know a single thing about Ligaya until after their first meeting. To Loreto Asis, her interesting personality and the physical attributes were enough. He had no other agenda in mind, except to win her.

"So, you are from the great State of Hawaii?" Loreto asked Ligaya just to start a conversation.

"Yes. But my work brings me to Washington D.C. once in a while," she replied as if to impress him.

"Well, what do you know. I have friends and relatives in Hawaii too. So, you must be active with the Democratic Party there, huh,"

Loreto replied fishing for an affirmative answer.

"Sorry, I am a Republican. My presence here is part of my work and partly because I am also a Filipino-American," answered Ligaya with an air of superiority.

"Great! I think we should really work together for the common good of Filipino-Americans" was the smart reply of Loreto, desperately trying to be positive and stay connected. Loreto was definitely smitten and being challenged by Ligaya.

They exchanged business cards and Loreto promised to call her to see how they can work together.

This was the start of a love affair between two Third-generation Filipino-Americans. The only common thing between them was their Filipino heritage. Politically Loreto was a Democrat. Ligaya was Republican. Loreto basically was a private executive and an entrepreneur. Ligaya was a government employee. Loreto was in all respect born and raised in America. Ligaya was born and raised in the Philippines.

But as the cliché goes, all is fair in love and in war. Loreto finally met his match.

CHAPTER 12

Returning to their Roots

"They and no Filipino-American ever have to be afraid to tell people of who they were and where they came from."

After the Washington D.C. conference, Loreto and Ligaya would become involved more deeply with their respective Filipino-American communities and with each other. Less than a year after they met, they got engaged and prepared for a Hawaiian wedding.

Loreto flew in to Honolulu to attend a town-hall meeting organized by the local

Democratic Party headed by the closely knit Ilocano Filipino-Americans of Hawaii. The Fil-ams of Hawaii did not call themselves Filipinos. They would prefer to call themselves Ilocanos. Their great grand parents who first came to Hawaii in the 1930s have not connected them back to their roots for so long that they could not really relate to Filipinos or even the Philippines. They could relate to their blood relatives and friends who were definitely Ilocanos. But mostly because they were all residents of Hawaii. Ilocanos in Hawaii are very clannish. Loreto, whether he knew that he had Ilocano blood or not, was wearing his Ilocano-race hat at the meeting. This was the reason why Ligaya Depuesto was also in the meeting. She was there because she is an Ilocana. That carries more weight than her being a Republican. Of course, she knew that Loreto was going to be there too as one of the guest speakers. The Ilocano block was consolidating their support behind fellow Ilocano Ben Cayetano, the current Lieutenant Governor who was making a run for the governorship of Hawaii in November 1994.

Loreto was the speaker before Ben Cayetano and he was supposed to build the excitement and hype-up the crowd by the time Cayetano speaks. He did a good job as his introduction of Cayetano was drowned out by a deafening noise made by the excited crowd. While Ben Cayetano was preparing to deliver his speech, Loreto made his way to where Ligaya was seating and whispered something in her ear. Hand-in-hand they made their way through the crowd and to the exit unnoticed. They hailed a cab and went to Waikiki Hilton Village Resort where the Society of Seven were performing.

Unknown to Ligaya, Loreto arranged beforehand a table for two in front of the stage where a bottle of Dom Perignon had been chilled, ready to be popped and poured on two tall glasses. Once seated, Ligaya could not contain herself and she was actually torn between staring at her idol Bert Nievera of the Society of Seven or thanking Loreto for the pleasant surprise.

“Loreto, this is too much!” was all Ligaya could say.

From the stage, Bert Nievera himself announced, “Ladies and gentlemen. This next song is for Miss Ligaya Depuesto and former

Mayor Loreto Asis of the City of Vallejo who are celebrating a very special occasion."

After they sang "The Seventh Dawn", the favorite song of Ligaya that was originally sung by the Lettermen, Loreto went down on his knees, took the ring out from his pocket and asked Ligaya, "Will you marry me?"

The crowd burst into a round of applause while the champagne bottle popped.

It was a happy if not a very complimentary union. Loreto would bring Ligaya to community events and activities dominated by Democrats while Ligaya would maintain her Republican ties for the purpose of facilitating favors for the Filipino-American community.

But the marriage really gave Loreto an opportunity to know and trace his roots that were kept secret from him by his grandfather and his father Arnulfo. Ligaya made it one of her priority projects, the *Filipinization* of Loreto.

As months and years went by and with the arrival of their only daughter Mutya in 1998, Loreto became more interested in involving himself with the Filipino-American communities and their issues. Loreto was determined to trace the roots of his grandfather from Pagudpud, Ilocos Norte and her grandmother, from Taft Eastern Samar.

The Filipinization of Loreto

In 1996, a popular Filipino-American weekly newspaper, The Manila Bulletin USA started organizing what became to be the largest Filipino-American summer festival in northern California, the Fiesta Filipina. This festival featured Filipino arts and culture in the form of music, dance, Filipino cultural presentations and of course food. It became an occasion and outlet for Filipinos in the Bay area to come together and celebrate the Philippine Independence Day during the month of June. Local talents from the Filipino-American communities like Rex Navarrete and Jaya started from the stage of Fiesta Filipina. The festival also featured the best and the most popular TV and movie personalities coming from Manila. It became a medium for the local young and older Filipino-Americans to show their talents and be connected as well to the latest art and music scene from the Philippines. The Fiesta attracted politicians, personalities and anybody who is somebody both from the Philippines and from the US mainland. A year before Carlos Santana won his second Grammy, his LP "Smooth" as Grammy's LP of the year, Santana volunteered to perform for free at the Centennial Celebration of the Philippine Independence Day at the 1998 edition of the Fiesta Filipina. More than 80,000 people came during the two-day celebration, young, old, white, black, yellow and brown to celebrate diversity.

Loreto and Ligaya have been steady supporters of the Fiesta since 1994. It was a very mutually productive and strategic relationship that gave Ligaya and Loreto a consistent link to the Filipino-American readers of the newspaper.

Being one of the regular supporters now of Filipino-American community events, Loreto proposed to sponsor a contest among Filipino-American 10th to 12th graders on Philippine history. The objective was to start interest among the young generation, the

Fourth Fil-Am or the Post-Millennial Fil-Am generation on Philippine history.

As envisioned, the contest would give young Fil-Ams an opportunity to know their Philippine roots by way of a quiz show in history. Each participating high school was to form a team composed of five team members each. The Philippine history quiz show competition attracted senior high schools in California and Hawaii.

At the finals held at the U.N. Plaza, San Francisco Civic Center edition of Fiesta Filipina in 1997, five lucky 12th graders from Honolulu, Hawaii beat ten other schools in the Bay Area and Los Angeles. Even those who did not win have increased their awareness of their Filipino heritage at the very least. The winners were treated to an all-expenses paid a five-day visit of historical places in Manila, courtesy of the Philippine Department of Tourism, the Philippine Charity Sweepstakes Office and of course the organizers of Fiesta Filipina.

It was easy for the youngest generation of Filipino-Americans to lose their connection to their roots because after 1997, they were being assimilated easily into the mainstream American society. Their grandparents if they were still alive would be in their late 70s, 80s or even 90s. When they die, they take with them the Filipino customs and traditions that they kept alive in the US when they were younger. Their parents who would be in their late 40s to 60s have been Americanized somewhat and will be just as confused or clueless as they were. This was the generation that Loreto Asis represented.

"If we could do this with our young generations, I think I should trace my own heritage myself!" Loreto told Ligaya and his Filipino friend and organizer of the Fiesta Filipina.

Thus, started the quest of Loreto to trace his Filipino ancestry that for so long was kept secret from him by his grandfather and father.

Back to Where it all Started, Returning to their Roots in Ilocos

With the help of Ligaya's relatives in Sta. Maria, Ilocos Sur, Ligaya and Loreto embarked on a trip to trace both their roots. Ligaya's father was from Sta. Maria, Ilocos

Sur where she grew up while her mother hailed from Dulag, Leyte.

Mutya, their only daughter would be 11 at this time and it will be her first time to visit the Philippines too. It was going to be Loreto's first time ever as well to visit the Philippines. Mutya, according to the newest generation classification tool Pew Research Center devised, is a Post-Millennial baby. These were those who were born from 1997 to the present.

The PR 105 Flight of Philippine Airlines was packed to the last seat. The flight from San Francisco to Manila will take nearly 14 hours, with a technical stop at either Honolulu or Guam. The shortest time would be 12 hours without a technical stop. Thanks to Loreto, the Asis family were on Business Class.

One of the most ubiquitous items one sees at the airport for Manila bound flights from the US and everywhere else, is the "Balikbayan box". The Balikbayan box is a square carton box, about 21"x21"x21" that is popularly used by returning Filipinos to ship their "pasalubongs" (gifts and presents) to their loved ones in the Philippines. Balikbayan is a fusion of two Filipino words: "Balik" (Return) and "Bayan" (Country) or "return-country". It is cheap, light, reusable if properly handled, otherwise it is also disposable. A regular travelling luggage would cost probably $100 upwards each and could only carry less stuff. A Balikbayan Box costs only about $10 to $15 dollars and could accommodate more as long as the total weight of each box does not exceed 23 kilos. Ligaya being a true Ilocana had three of these packed, in addition to their two pieces each of their Samsonite check in and cabin luggage.

At the Philippine Air Lines check-in counter, Mutya was secretly protesting to her dad, while Ligaya was busy presiding over the tagging of their luggage.

"Dad, why are we carrying so much stuff? Who is going to carry these boxes out when we check out of the airport? I'm not touching those, dad," Mutya emphatically told her intention to her dad.

Bewildered and not knowing also how things would be, Loreto turns to Ligaya for answers.

"So how do we take care of all these boxes and our luggage? Will there be porters at the baggage carousels in Manila?" Loreto asked Ligaya.

"Oh, that is not a problem. My dad arranged for everything. There will be someone at immigration who will meet us," Ligaya answered without looking at Loreto as her eyes were fixed on the boxes that were still being tagged and labelled.

That was very reassuring for both the 11-year-old Mutya and her dad but thinking about the next 12 hours ahead of them, both dad and daughter were not very optimistic.

"Twelve hours dad! Can we just stop at Honolulu first? We have friends and relatives there anyway," Mutya continued to protest.

Mom and dad looked at each other, and Ligaya answered in English but in hard Ilocano accent, "It is going to be okay because you can sleep during the flight. We are at Business Class anyway. Besides staying in Honolulu is an unnecessary expense and we are expected to arrive in Manila as scheduled."

The flight went well and before they know it, the purser woke everyone up to prepare for breakfast because they will be landing in three hours.

"What's for breakfast?" Mutya asked her mom.

"A choice of longanisa or beef tapa or smoked milkfish with egg and fried rice," replied Ligaya.

"Can I have cereals, bacon and scrambled eggs?" Mutya asked again.

"Honey, this is not a restaurant, choose what is in the airline menu," was the emphatic reply of Ligaya.

As soon as they landed at the Ninoy Aquino International Airport, the pilot made an announcement.

"Welcome to Manila, Philippines. I hope you had a pleasant flight. Thank you for choosing Philippine Airlines, the first in Asia," blared the public address.

Proceeding to the Philippine Immigration, the lines were long as more than 600 passengers from two other flights were waiting to be processed with only four immigration officers on duty. It was about 4:30 am of the following day. One loses a day returning to the Philippines but gains a day returning back to the US.

True enough, someone with an all-access security tag emerged behind one of the counters and held a up sign across his chest "LIGAYA DEPUESTO ASIS".

"That's for us," Ligaya happily told her husband and daughter.

"Ma'am and sir, kindly step out of the line and just follow me," said the man politely.

He took their passports, tickets and luggage tags, and led them to the luggage carousel where two other guys were waiting to pick up their luggage.

Loreto was smiling but a little bit embarrassed that they cut through the long lines but at the same time very relieved by the help.

"It's okay. That is how things are done here. Nobody will complain," explained Ligaya.

Loreto was in fact amused that really, nobody complained when they cut and skipped the line. People were smiling and some seemed even impressed at the privilege given to them.

"Wow, I might really like it here now," Loreto exclaimed as they were ushered into a waiting airconditioned limo, with their boxes and luggage carried for them by smiling fellows.

This was just the beginning of the adventure that awaits the Asis family, particularly first-time visitors Loreto and daughter Mutya.

Sta. Maria, Ilocos Sur

The Asis spent the day resting at the Century Park Hotel in Ermita, Manila before their road trip to Sta. Maria, Ilocos Sur. They booked three first Class tickets at the Farinas Bus Lines for the midnight departure for Sta. Maria, Ilocos Sur. They were going to travel all night and arrive at Sta. Maria before noon.

Right on the dot, the air-conditioned bus was parking at the Sta. Maria bus terminal at about 11:40 am. A black

Esplanade SUV was already waiting at the terminal when they arrived. Mr. Depuesto now in the 80s and who is not able to move around so much, was waiting at their house in población, right next to the Basilica. The house is a restored Spanish era house. Not a mansion by Spanish standards but it is big and spacious enough to accommodate comfortably more than one family.

In the Philippines, especially in the towns once established by the Spaniards, the location of the house indicates one's position in society. The higher or more important the person is, the closest his house will be to the church and the municipal building. The church would occupy the highest ground level, followed by the municipal building. The Depuesto residence was right across the municipal hall.

The visiting Asises were treated to authentic Ilocano cuisine of "caldereta, papaitan, bagnet, kinilaw and pinakbet". Caldereta is a Spanish inspired goat meat stew in red sauce, olives and pepper. Papaitan is a soup made from the goat's bile and blood. It is not for everyone but Ilocanos love this dish. Bagnet is a slab of pork sides deep fried in boiling oil until it becomes very crunchy. Kinilaw on the other hand is the basted and pickled skin of the goat, steeped in vinegar, black pepper, garlic, onions, hot pepper and ginger. All these dishes are best eaten as "pulutan" and are washed down by a local wine made from sugarcane juice – "basi." Pulutan is whatever food was on the table when the Ilocanos are drinking alcoholic beverages. Pinakbet is a vegetable dish made from sautéed bitter melon, eggplant, string beans, squash and sometimes green beans. The Ilocanos use either "bagoong" from fish or shrimp to season it. Bagoong is a very salty pickled and fermented fish or shrimp.

Driving around town for the first time, Loreto and Mutya saw a sample of Filipino mechanical ingenuity. They saw the Ilocano version of the "Habal-habal". The Habal-habal is a modified motorcycle designed to carry up to eight passengers, including the driver of the motorcycle. A couple of seats are placed on top of the gas tank in front, plus the extended rear to accommodate four more. To carry the extra weight, two pairs of shock absorbers are fitted both in front and at the extended rear. The Filipino just expanded the capacity of a 250-c.c. motorcycle from two to seven passengers. Even the Japanese who built these motorcycles are amazed whenever they see one. The added capacity made-up for the lack of units of motorcycles in the more remote areas of the Philippines.

Relaxing at the Depuesto house, "This is where my family came from," Ligaya proudly exclaimed to both Loreto and Mutya.

"Do you have internet?" Mutya asked, not paying attention to her mom's story.

"We have at the internet shop near the grocery," one of the aunties obligingly replied. "But only at certain times of the day," she continued.

"Do you have cable?" Mutya continued to badger.

At this, Ligaya told her daughter, "We did not come here to watch cable! So please stop asking."

Loreto now understood why Macario did not want Ligaya to go to the US. What for? They have everything here in Sta. Maria.

Status, convenience and they are financially well-off.

After a week of visiting relatives and the old churches in Paoay and Vigan and the beaches of Pagudpud, Ilocos Norte, they were ready to go south to Tacloban City, Leyte and Samar. In Pagudpud, Loreto took samples of the fine white sand, musing at the thought of visiting his grandfather's origin. It was an amazing place he thought.

The Leyte Landing and Dulag Shrines

"What could be a more appropriate time to visit the Philippines and trace our roots at Dulag, Leyte and Samar than doing it on Octobe19 to 26, during the celebration of the Anniversary of the Leyte Landings and the Battle of Leyte?" declared Ligaya Depuesto Asis when they first planned the trip, months earlier.

"We can't. Mutya has to go back to school in September," replied Loreto. They were not meant to visit during the fall.

So, the family took the sentimental journey to their roots during the summer of

2010. They were now about to come face to face with their past in Palo and Dulag, Leyte.

From Manila, the flight to the Daniel Z. Romualdez airport in Tacloban City was just one hour. The approach to the runway of the Tacloban airport in San Jose afforded a beautiful view of the city and the San Juanico bridge. One could also see the jagged edges of the mountains and ridges that separated the north-eastern part with the north-western part of the island. The airport runway juts out of the San Pedro Bay like a thumb from Cataisan and Barangay San Jose of Tacloban City. Without the shanties or houses on both sides of the road leading to the airport terminal, one would have a beautiful view of both Kankabato and San Pedro Bays. The only time one had this opportunity to see both bays from the airport road was right after super-typhoon Haiyan (Yolanda) wiped out all the structures on both sides of the road.

Both Loreto and Ligaya were having goose-bumps as the plane gently touched down, made a U-turn at the end of the short runway and slowly taxied to its designated place at the tarmac. There was no tube gangway so they disembarked from the plane and walked out to the open, and into the terminal.

The airport was much smaller than the NAIA International Airport but it was busy. Since 2010 there were now 16 flights every day to Tacloban City from Manila, Cebu, Iloilo and back. Tacloban City is the gateway to the six provinces of Eastern Visayas (Leyte, Southern Leyte, Eastern Samar, Northern Samar, Samar and Biliran).

They checked in at the old Hotel Alejandro on Burgos Street. This hotel used to be the old Montejo mansion where Ligaya's father and mother had their honeymoon. The place had been kept well and restored to almost the original state, except for the closing of large windows so it could be airconditioned.

The second floor of the old pavilion is now like a museum of sorts. Along the corridors hung the enlarged black and white pictures of the Leyte landings. As Ligaya and Loreto gazed at the pictures, vivid memories of the past seem to float around their consciousness, as if hypnotizing and freezing both of them.

"Mom. Dad!" cried Mutya as she brought both of them back to their senses.

"The room boy said that they now have a mall in Tacloban. Can we go to Macdonald's and then the mall at Robinson's Place?" Mutya pleaded.

"Let us go first to Palo to see the Leyte Landings Shrine. Then you can have your burger downtown," Ligaya assured her daughter.

Next stop was the Palo Shrine of the landing. As their van parked in front of the shrine, a couple of vendors hawking their balut and peanuts immediately accosted Loreto.

"Balut sir. Pang-kusog han tuhod," said the one selling balut. (Eat balut sir, so you will have strong legs.)

"What's balut?" Loreto asked Ligaya.

"Oh, balut is a nine to twelve-day old embryo from duck egg. They boil it and you eat it from its shell," explained Ligaya.

"Would you like to try? It's a Filipino delicacy and they say it is some kind of an aphrodisiac," Ligaya naughtily added to her explanation.

"Really?" Loreto replied raising his eyebrows.

"Embryos? That is really gross!" Mutya interjected as they made their way to the ten-feet tall statues of the Leyte landing shrine.

The larger than life depiction of General MacArthur, President Sergio Osmena, Gen. Carlos P. Romulo, two aides and Macario Depuesto wading at the knee-high waters of the Red beach brought tears in Ligaya's eyes. Loreto was speechless.

"Which one is my Lolo?" Mutya innocently asked her mom.

Ligaya pointed to the statue of a man at the far right and rear of the group.

"Uh oh. I do not think so. He is too tall and ugly," Mutya corrected her mom.

Loreto could not stop laughing at this but a sharp stare from Ligaya stopped him on his track.

Visiting Dulag for the first Time

The Tacloban City trip was the first for everybody, including Ligaya. She was from Ilocos and she never visited Leyte before. Not even Macario would come to visit. The town of Dulag was just a thirty to forty minute-drive from Tacloban, northeast of the city. The center of the town is about three kilometers from the shores where the American liberating forces landed. The small municipal hall is facing a public plaza where the statue of Jose Rizal stood in the middle. But farther down at the northern corner of the plaza was another monument. It was a monument of a Japanese Officer, complete with a sabre and hat. In front of the base of the statue read a plaque:

"Captain Hideki Yamaguchi, Officer and Gentleman, Japanese Imperial Army"

Ligaya was quiet but deep thoughts of what could have been played around with her imagination. This is the statue of the man her mom first fell in love with. There was nothing like this anywhere else in the Philippines, where a former enemy was given tribute. But to Ligaya, the anomaly was more than that.

Loreto was also quiet, but in his mind, it occurred to him that he may not have met Ligaya if this man and his mother-in-law got married instead of Macario. Also, he was amazed that this town which was liberated by the Americans from the Japanese has a statue honoring the enemy. They do not even have a plaque of appreciation for the Americans!

For Mutya, she wanted to say “This is so boring!” but it was just her silent thought.

Finally, she spoke, “Mom, dad, where will we eat for lunch?”

Lunch was at Max Restaurant at Robinson’s place at Marasbaras. Max is a family restaurant started in the 50s by a family from Quezon city, specializing in its juicy and crispy fried spring chicken. Mutya was looking for a McDonalds’ store at the mall but was disappointed because there was none. The mall had only Jollibee, the local but very popular burger joint that somehow mastered and captured the “Filipino” taste-bud for spaghetti and its burgers.

"So, what is your impression of Tacloban City?" Ligaya asked Loreto back in their room at Hotel Alejandro.

"Interesting." Loreto replied.

"Like how interesting?" Ligaya followed through.

"Well, for one thing, downtown Tacloban is really nothing but a big Chinatown. There are many interesting places in the city but they have not been discovered yet by visitors, for lack of information and exposure. They should do a lot better in taking care of their heritage assets in this town. However, it is amazing how these Tacloban Chinese were totally assimilated into the local culture and community. They speak the dialect well and have taken ownership of the local culture and the city," Loreto replied to Ligaya in genuine amazement. He came upon this observation after talking to some shop owners and Mr. Montejo himself, the proprietor of the hotel.

"If there is any ethnic-group we all should learn from, it should be from the Filipino-Chinese of Tacloban City. They have totally embraced the culture, the language and even the food without forgetting their own," continued Loreto.

"No wonder, many of them are successful and they can thrive in places foreign to them, including in America," said Loreto.

"But I do not understand, so please tell me Ligaya. Why the heck is Eastern Visayas the second poorest region in the Philippines, just ahead of the Muslim Mindanao? Goodness, they have everything here! They do not look poor at all." Loreto asked Ligaya puzzled and mystified.

"Wow. You noticed all that in just a few days visit here?" Ligaya replied still amazed and in total agreement with Loreto.

Touching the Soil and Kissing the ground at Samar

Loreto's father was born in Hawaii. But her grandmother Mana Yolanda originally came from a small fishing town now called Taft, Eastern Samar. The following day, the family was driven from Tacloban City to Samar via the beautiful San Juanico bridge. The 2.2-kilometer bridge crosses over the San Juanico Strait, one of the most beautiful straits in the world. It is also one of the most treacherous, with its fast current, narrow navigating alley for ships to pass and its sand bars on both sides of the strait.

Upon reaching the other end of the bridge on the Samar side, Loreto asked the driver to stop so he could step out. He went down on his knees touched the soil and kissed the ground. This was where the Asis came from. For the first time ever, a descendant of Yolanda Cinco and Manoling Asis is standing on Samar soil. This was an emotional time for the family. Even Mutya seemed to have understood the poignancy of the occasion.

Loreto was relieved at the thought that finally, he has retraced his roots and that he did not have to apologize to anyone for his family's origins. He wanted to visit his grandparent's tombs back in Hawaii to tell them how proud he was that he is also a Filipino-American whose grandparents came from very humble beginnings.

They and no Filipino-American ever have to be afraid to tell people of who they were and where they came from.

EPILOGUE

The stories of the families of Macario Depuesto, Dalisay Borja and Loreto Asis represent the generations of Filipino-Americans who helped build America. Among Asians these Filipino-Americans made their quiet contributions without deliberately inviting attention and honor to themselves.

Thanks to the customs and traditions and the culture that the first and second generations brought with them to America, the third generation Filipino-Americans (or Fil-ams for short) held on to these, their only remaining connections with the Philippines, their country of origin. They did this not only for the love of their heritage but probably more so to survive the adverse social, political and economic environment that the two earlier generations were also exposed to as immigrants of ethnic origin.

Macario Depuesto's parents, Manong Julian and Manang Unding as well as the parents of Arnulfo Asis, Manong Manoling and Mana Yolanda were among the poorest of the poor of the Filipino rice, tobacco and coconut farmers that comprised the majority of the Philippine population. This was the case in the 1930s when they started immigrating to America to pursue the "American Dream".

Unfortunately, today nearly ninety years later, in spite of the economic "progress" the Philippines has achieved after the war and the political independence from the US in 1946, their kind, the Filipino farmers are still among the poorest of the poor! Of the unofficial estimated 108.285 million Filipinos today, at least 23.390 million or 21.6% (as of 2019) are just barely breaking through the new and "revised" poverty line as defined by the Philippine Statistics Authority. According to the Philippine Statistics Agency (PSA), the poverty income threshold in 2018 is now at about PHP 12,500 a month, or about $250.00 at PHP50:$1.00. Yet we could not deny that the Philippines, under the guidance and by virtue (or in spite of, if you agree with the more progressive thinking Filipinos) of its "special relations" with America, is now enjoying unprecedented economic growth.

With its GDP per capita income estimated at US$3,729.55, said to be at its historical highest, (even if this is only about 23% of the world's average and therefore considered poor by international standards) the Philippines is now among the top ten fast growing economies of Southeast Asia, including Japan, Taiwan, Singapore, South Korea, Hongkong and China. The Standards and Poor and other international credit bureaus, not to mention the International Monetary Fund (IMF) and the Asian Development Bank (ADB) have upgraded the Philippine credit rating to BBB+ since it drastically fell during the Marcos regime and shortly before the EDSA Mutiny in 1986 (more popularly called the first People's Power Revolution in Asia). This meant the country is just a notch away from being A-, but already is in the "investment grade" territory.

But why is there so much poverty still in the Philippines? The reason for this is not as complex as it may seem. The economic progress has not filtered down to the lowest levels of the Philippine economic classes. The higher per capita incomes do not reflect the very unequal distribution of wealth in the

Philippines. Vestiges of the feudalistic and "padrino" systems that were encouraged and nurtured by the Spaniards and to some extent by the Americans for more than a century, are still undermining our political institutions. These, along with bad patronage politics have been the bane of the Filipino people. They have been the barnacles that weakened the foundations of a society lacking in social and economic mobility. They were largely responsible for the existence of economic deprivation among the masses in the Philippines even before Macario's and Dalisay's parents were born. These were the same barriers that continue to deny the Filipino farmer, or the "common man" from enjoying the gains of economic progress after the Second World War. If it is a consolation (or a worry), the gap between the rich and the poor in America and the rest of the more affluent countries also increased, according to some economists. Finally, this was the same reason for the phenomenon of the Filipino diaspora all over the world. Lack of opportunities at home forced Filipinos to leave the country and look for job opportunities elsewhere. This actually started as early as when the Americans colonized the country in the 1900s. It started long before Ferdinand Marcos came to power in the Philippines. Through the power of American television and the magic of Hollywood, America and their way of life became every Filipino's dream, just like how Ligaya Depuesto became obsessed by it.

The former enemies got a better deal

The former enemies, Japan and Germany, it turned out, both got a better deal from the Americans. The "Marshall Plan" or better known as the post-war rehabilitation of Western Europe was implemented. It involved the spending of an estimated hundred billion dollars of economic aid to Western Europe. The rest was history. Germany and the rest of Europe rose from the ashes of war to economic power that they are still known today. With the help of Gen. MacArthur's leadership at the Supreme Command of Allied Powers (SCAP), Japan's government and society were reformed and transformed. Japan was disarmed and rid of its former war hawks. With the cooperation of Emperor Hirohito and billions of dollars of rehabilitation aid from the US and its Allies, Japan became one of the world's largest economies in the 1970s, behind America, Germany, Great Britain and France. Japan became a member of the elite "Group of 7".

The Rescission Act of 1946

What an ironic turn of events one might say. The Philippines, ever loyal and faithful to America seemed to have gotten a raw deal. Immediately after the war, under the Democratic Whitehouse the infamous Recission Act of 1946 was passed. According to Wikipedia, the Rescission Act of 1946 (38 U.S.C. § 107), *"is a law of the United States that retroactively annulled benefits that would have been payable to Filipino troops on account of their military service under the auspices the United States during the time that the Philippines was a U.S. territory and Filipinos were U.S. nationals."* The bill was first vetoed by President Truman on its introduction. But irony of ironies, this anti-Filipino bill that easily passed into law on second filing was sponsored by Democrats, Senator Carl Hayden of Arizona and Senator

Richard B. Russel, Jr. of Georgia. Both conservatives also opposed the Civil rights movement in the 60s. As if to redeem themselves, the law that repealed this unjust act, was sponsored in 2008 by Senator Daniel K. Inoue, a Democrat. But this was after a long-drawn fight by Filipino-Americans and the support of the more understanding American public. It was only as late as 2016 and about 63 years later, that President Barack Obama, signed into law a bipartisan bill sponsored by Mike Thompson (California) and Tom Udall (New Mexico) both Democrats.

This was the Congressional Medal of Honor Award to Filipinos who fought the Second World War alongside the Americans. By then, of the 200,000 Filipino World War Veterans eligible for the award, only about 15,000 were still alive. Among them was Sotero L. Palabyab of San Jose Del Monte, Bulacan, veteran of the Death March in Capas, Tarlac in 1942. 2nd Lieutenant Rufino L. Palabyab of the Bulacan guerillas who lost his wife, siblings and mother from a direct-hit by a B-24 bomb and hundreds of others who similarly lost their loved ones during the carpet bombing of Manila and Central Luzon during the liberation of the Philippines in January, 1945 did not receive its financial benefits, simply because they died before 2008. By then the grant of the posthumous honor was already meaningless for the widows and orphans of dead Filipino war veterans.

This was how America treated one of its most loyal allies in the second world war. With friends like this, who needs an enemy? But the reality is that there are no permanent friends or allies, only permanent interests. Everything that happened and are still to happen to the rest of the free-world, friend or foe will be according to the dictates of American economic and military interests.

Mutya Depuesto Asis, Post Millennial Filipino-American

Mutya Asis, now 19, is on her 2nd year at UC Berkeley, taking up Political Science and Asian Studies. She has gone a long way since their family's first visit to their roots in the Philippines about eight years earlier. All Mutya could think of then, was where she could find a reliable internet connection, or where she could follow her favorite MTV and

Disney channels on cable TV. She definitely likes Netflix, Twitter, Facebook and Instagram but now she is also reading The Economist and Balikbayan Magazine whenever she can and in-between listening to her iPhone 10 podcasts. She loves her Philippine cousins and friends whom she regularly talks to on Viber and Messenger but there's just too many things to get busy with in school and her social life. She goes out with everybody. Black, white, yellow or brown, the color of his skin does not really matter as long as he is a cool guy and not a criminal. And her parents, whether they approve or not cannot do anything about it. She is 19 now, but still lives with her parents Loreto and Ligaya. That is the only reason why she has to follow rules in the house and the Asis standard code of conduct outside the house. Besides, her parents are still paying for her tuition at UC Berkeley.

Loreto told Mutya to read the "Untold and Unending Coconut Story", a paper originally presented to the NaFFAA assembly during the first empowerment conference in Washington DC in 1997 by Filipino-American associations. At that time, the most pressing initiative on hand was the Philippine Veterans Equity initiative that repealed the Recission Act. It galvanized the Filipino-American communities all over America. Now that it had been won, Loreto suggested to Mutya to look at this other paper that might unify and rally the Fil Ams again. Of late there had been bickering and division due to divergent beliefs on issues obtaining in the Philippines. The Duterte administration's alleged "extra judicial killings" have divided the Fil-ams among others. They needed a unifying cause to galvanize them again just like the Veterans Equity initiative did. Loreto thinks that the US Coconut levy that was passed with the US Revenue Act of 1935 was just as pernicious to the Filipino coconut farmers as the Recission Act was to the Filipino veteran.

The Revenue Act of 1935 was passed by the US Congress at the instance of the American dairy farmers and Soybean oil producers who wanted to "kill" the Philippine coconut industry by levying a tariff that was 200% of its prevailing export price to the US, without regard to the untold hardship it would cause the Filipino people. During the Philippine Commonwealth period, up to eighty per cent of the farmers' livelihood were derived from coconut farming. The law was never repealed and the collection of the levy continued even after 1946, when the Laurel-Langley Treaty went into effect. After the Philippine independence was granted, the Laurel-Langley treaty clearly outlawed the US coconut levy under its "Trade Parity Clause". The writer of the paper believed that the US government owed the Philippines and its coconut farmers billions of US dollars from excise tax levies illegally collected and the accumulated interest from 1946 to 1966 when the collection was finally stopped. Loreto and Ligaya gave Mutya the assignment of researching on this in preparation for the next NaFFAA conference and as a paper she could submit in her Political Science course at UC Berkeley.

Meanwhile, the American society has evolved and changed so much during the last fifty years. The face of America has changed so much as well. The new breed of Americans is changing the way people talk (as in political correctness) and perhaps the way they should be represented physically. Truly America is now a melting pot, not only of Anglo-Saxons but more so for people of color. The Asians and the Latinos are the fastest growing ethnic minorities in America today. Even the American Barbie doll has undergone changes. No longer is she the blond white skinny doll of the 60s and 70s. You can now get black and brown skinned Barbie dolls.

But it will still take a few more generations if ever they want to change Uncle Sam's face too. The whites are getting fewer and fewer in terms of their relative numbers. But they are still the majority. They may not be breeding as fast as the ethnic minorities but they are very much still in control of America. He who has the gold shall also have the guns and therefore power. Although there are more billionaires in America than any other economy, the same old-rich families generally dominate the super-rich in America. The super-elites of the American society remain Anglo-Saxon. Life goes on. Filipinos in the Philippines and in America are still in pursuit of that elusive American dream.

For the Depuestos and the Asises, they already have the best of both worlds

ABOUT THE AUTHOR

GERMAN P. PALABYAB

Mr. Palabyab spent fourteen years in the US (1987-2001) as an educator and a journalist in San Francisco, Bay area, editing and publishing a Filipino-American weekly newspaper, producing a weekly tele-magazine on KTSF Channel 26, producing Fiesta Filipina, the largest Filipino-American Summer Festival in northern California, and teaching at the West Contra Costa Unified School District.

Mr. Palabyab was among the original charter members of the National Federation of Filipino-American Associations, NaFFAA (1997, Washington DC), the umbrella organization of all Filipino-American associations in continental US and the Hawaiian Islands. The NaFFAA grew to become the recognized federation of Filipino-

American associations by the US government after its inception in 1997.

His writings on the saga and continuing story of the Philippine coconut industry and Philippine history in general started in 1997 when he submitted a discussion paper for consideration during the First NaFFAA Filipino-American Empowerment Conference held in August 1997 in Washington D.C. It was also the eve of the celebration of the centennial of RP-US relations (1898-1998) and Mr. Palabyab was also quietly drawn into what they called the "history-wars" that was held in San Francisco in 1998 featuring the discussion of many untold and little known historical events that were deliberately or inadvertently omitted by historians during the last 100 years. The Balanggica Massacre and the Coconut Story were just two among several "controversial" topics for discussion.

There was a reason why the author was particularly drawn to stories about the liberation of the Philippines. During the liberation of Manila in January, 1945, Mr. Palabyab's paternal grandparent's house in San Jose Del Monte, Bulacan was hit by a bomb from an American B-24 bomber, that killed his grandmother, two siblings of his father and his father's first wife. His father, Rufino L. Palabyab, M.D., who was a 1st Lieutenant of a Bulacan Guerilla Unit of WWII said that, the hardest thing for him was to watch his wife, his mother, elder sister and brother slowly die from their wounds as he was also severely wounded and was barely alive after the bomb hit.

This historical fiction (*The Saga of Leyte Gulf*) was the synthesis all his research on the many untold or "mis-told" stories that involved our American colonizers since 1898. Mr. Palabyab opted to write a historical fiction, in order to dramatize actual historical events without being hampered by the need to document sources of information. Many of the folktales and "stories" were gathered by oral interview owing to the lack of proper written records on many of the anecdotes during the Japanese occupation and liberation of the Philippines.

Made in the USA
Monee, IL
20 January 2023